A.A. Smets

Catalogue of the Private Collection of Autographs of the late Mr. A.A. Smets

A.A. Smets

Catalogue of the Private Collection of Autographs of the late Mr. A.A. Smets

Reprint of the original, first published in 1868.

1st Edition 2022 | ISBN: 978-3-37501-316-5

Verlag (Publisher): Salzwasser Verlag GmbH, Zeilweg 44, 60439 Frankfurt, Deutschland
Vertretungsberechtigt (Authorized to represent): E. Roepke, Zeilweg 44, 60439 Frankfurt, Deutschland
Druck (Print): Books on Demand GmbH, In de Tarpen 42, 22848 Norderstedt, Deutschland

CATALOGUE

OF THE

PRIVATE COLLECTION OF

AUTOGRAPHS

OF THE LATE

Mr. A. A. SMETS, of Savannah, Ga.

COMPRISING

A CHOICE ASSORTMENT OF RARE AUTOGRAPH LETTERS, EARLY MANUSCRIPTS, &c., &c.

ALSO,

A COLLECTION OF AUTOGRAPHS

Purchased from the Library of WILLIAM UPCOTT, consisting of 2,069 Autographs bound in 31 Volumes, 8vo, half calf.
With rare Portraits, &c.

THE WHOLE TO BE SOLD BY AUCTION,

AT THE

Clinton Hall Book Sale Rooms and Art Galleries,

LEAVITT, STREBEIGH & CO., Auctioneers,

MONDAY, JUNE 1st, AND FOLLOWING DAYS,

Commencing at 4 o'clock P.M. each day.

Gentlemen unable to attend the Sale can have their orders to purchase carefully attended to by the Auctioneers.

Catalogue.

 DAM (Sir W.) Oculist   *A N S*

2 ADDISON (Joseph). UNPUBLISHED POEMS, in his Autograph. 4to, *calf, gilt*

> On the fly-leaf are the signatures of ' Cha: Warwick,' and Charlotte Addison: the elegant essayist having married, August 2d, 1716, Charlotte, Countess of Warwick, grand-daughter of Sir Orlando Bridgman. The first poem in the book is entitled ' Van's House, built from the ruins of White Hall,' written in 1703, referring to the new play-house in the Hay-market. The minor poems are: ' Upon Love;' ' When will thy heart grow tender?' written in 1715, during his courtship; for Addison experienced more than the common share of a lover's difficulties in obtaining a bride—and more than a common share of a lover's disappointments in retaining her; ' Love's a Dream.' ' To Mr. Pope, on his second subscription to Homer;' ' A Riddle upon Coals;' ' Death makes all equal;' ' A Riddle upon a Shadow;' ' Apollo once to Venus sued;' a beautiful Apologue on Love, in the autograph of his daughter, who writes in the margin, ' Papa's work;' and an inscription upon the tomb of Edward Henry, Earl of Warwick and Holland, who died August 15, 1721, aged 24 years.
>
> There are various other Verses and Poems of 1726, and later, by Mrs. Madden. Songs to the tune of ' Under the Greenwood Tree,' etc., etc. Most of the Poems are written in a beautiful clear hand, one on the death of the ' Young Earl of Warwick,' and others by Addison's daughter, who writes in the margin *Papa's Works*. See Catalogue Raisonné, p. 15.

3 ADOLPHUS (John). Author. *A L S* 4to   1806

4 ALBUM AMICORUM FAMILIARUM ALARDI ET FABRICII. Containing numerous drawings, some of which are very spirited and curious. Autographs of different learned personages, etc. Oblong, 4to. *Original morocco binding, gilt edges.*   1624–56

> This is a valuable Album or common-place book, containing many extraordinary specimens of caligraphy, and including verses by (or

the autographs of) many distinguished literary persons of that time—Frederick Spanheim, 1645, John Fabricius, 1645, George Crasius, 1656, Petrus Lotichius, John Schmidt, 1635, George Mylius, 1635, Matthias Nicolai, 1634, Daniel Zwicker, 1635, Thomas Lindemannus, etc., etc.

Some of the drawings are very curious : in one Luther and Calvin are disputing, the Pope standing by and laughing; there are also divers emblematical devices, armorial bearings, etc.

The volume is very closely and beautifully written, and contains a great deal of matter. Among the Poetry are some German verses on King Charles the First, etc. It came from the Van Septem Collection, and sold at that sale for fourteen guineas. See Catalogue Raisonné, p. 14.

5 ALBUM OF A MUSICAL CLUB in Belgium. *Dated* 1581, 1583 *and* 1584. Small oblong quarto, *half bound, morocco.*

It contains the regulations of the Club, a discourse on music, poetry in its praise, etc., all in Latin ; also the signatures of the numerous members, with the coats of arms, in colors, of thirteen of them.

6 ALBUM OF ERNRICUS STAUFFER. Containing about 70 Autographs of Illustrious Personages, English and Foreign, with Sentences and Mottoes attached, in Hebrew, Greek, Latin, German, French, Spanish and Persian, also a few exquisite drawings, two emblazoned coats of arms, etc. Small oblong, 12mo, *in old morocco, gilt edges.* 1632–1640

This pretty little volume contains some beautiful specimens of caligraphy as well as the autographs of many celebrated persons. Among these are Frederick, Duke of Wurtemberg, dated 1640 : John Count of Hainault, 1633; John Freinshemius, the celebrated scholar, 1633 ; Saint George, 1634 ; Carolus de Montigni, 1633 ; Matthias Bernegger, 1634 ; Conrad Withmar, London, 1633 ; George Stewart, 1633 ; Steven and John Lingelshemius, 1633 ; Henry Harrison, Anglicus Cantabrigiensis, 1633 ; J. Podensteiner, Cambridge, 1633 ; Daniel Erastus Hurmobrodensis, Cambridge, 1633 ; J. W. Sartorius, 1633 ; also some foreign potentate signed Paul Frederic, 1633, and others. See Catalogue Raisonné, p. 14.

7 ALMONTÉ (J. N.) *A L S* 2 pp., 4to

8 ANSON (Ann Margaret). Daughter of Thos. W. Coke, Earl of Leicester. *A L S*

9 ANSON (Thomas), Viscount. Born 1767, died 1818.
A N S

10 ANTHON (John). *A N S*

11 ARNOLD (Samuel), Dramatist *A N* 3d person

12 AUSTEN (Mrs. Sarah). Authoress. *A L* 4 pp., 12mo

13 AUTOGRAPH PORTFOLIO (The). A collection of Fac-Simile Letters from Eminent Persons. 4to, *cloth*
London, 1838

14 AUTOGRAPHS OF ROYAL, NOBLE, LEARNED AND REMARKABLE Personages, conspicuous in English History, from the Reign of Richard the Second to that of Charles the Second, with some Illustrious Foreigners. Containing many passages from important Letters. Engraved under the direction of Charles John Smith. Accompanied by concise Biographical Memoirs, and interesting Extracts from Original Documents. By John Gough Nichols. 4to, *cloth*
London, 1829

15 BAINES (Edward), M.P. *A L S* 3 pp., 12mo
Portrait

16 BAIRD (Geo. H.) *A N S*

17 BANCROFT (Dr. Ed. Nathl.) Medical Writer. *A N S*

18 BANCROFT (George). Historian. *A L S.* Small 4to. *Mounted*.

19 BANNISTER (John). Celebrated Comedian. *A N S.*
Character Portrait. 1821

20 BARKER (Jacob). Known as one of the greatest Financiers of America. *A L S.* 1807

21 BARNUM (P. T.) Letter relating to his Autobiography *A L S.* 4to 1854

— 22 BARRETT (Miss E. B.) Poetess. *A N.* 3d person.

23 BARRINGTON (Hon. and Right Rev. Shute). Bishop of Durham. *A N.* 3d person.

24 BARRINGTON (Viscount). *A N.* 3d person.

25 BARROW (Sir John). Secretary to the Lords of Admiralty. *A L S.* 2 pp-folio.

26 BASSANO (Duc de). Ministre de Finance, Court of Napoleon Bonaparte. *L S. Very rare.* 1812

27 BATES (Barnabas). Known as the first advocate of the "Cheap Postage System." *A L S.* 2 pp. 4to.

28 BAYLEY (J.) Author. *A L S.* 12mo, 3 pp.

29 BAYLEY (Thomas Haynes). *A L S.* 3 pp, small 4to.

30 BEECHEY (Sir Wm.) R.A. Eminent Portrait Painter. *A N S.*

31 BENGER (Miss E. O.) Authoress of various Works. *A L S.*

32 BERTRAND (Gen.) Grand Marshal under Napoleon. *A N S.* 3d person. 20th Nov., 1811

33 BIDDLE (Wm.) *A L S.* 4to. 1835

34 BLAIR (Dr. Wm.) Surgeon. *A L S.*

35 BLISS (Major W. W. S.) Aid to Gen. Taylor and Asst.-Adjt.-Gen. in the Mexican War. *A L S.* 4to.

36 BONAPARTE (Napoleon, Emperor of France). *L S.* Bonaparte to the Minister of Finance. *Very good order—rare.*

37 BONAPARTE (Napoleon, Emperor of France). Letter signed as Emperor, commanding a New Report from the Counsellor of State. *L S* in cypher. June 6th, 1807

38 BONAPARTE (Joseph). King of Spain. *A L S.* 4to. *With portrait.*

39 BONAPARTE (Lucien). President of the Council of Five Hundred. *L S.*

40 BONAPARTE (Louis). King of Holland. *L S. With Portrait and Plate.*

41 BONAPARTE (Jerome). King of Westphalia. *L S. With Portrait.*

42 BOUCICAULT (Dion). To W. B. Hodgson of Savannah, Georgia. *A N S.*

43 BOURBON (Louis Jean Marie de). Duc de Penthièvre. The last heir of the legitimate Sons of Louis XIV. *A L S.*, 1785

44 BOWLES (W. L.) Poet. *A L S.* 3 pp., 4to.

45 BOWRING (Dr. John). Author. *A N S. Portrait.*

46 BREWER (James Norris). Miscellaneous Writer. *A L S.* 2 pp., 12mo. 1820

47 BREWSTER'S (Sir David), Optics. Original Manuscript in the Author's Autograph, not complete. 4to, *half calf.*

— 48 BRIDGMAN (Laura). "Deaf, dumb and blind since 12 months of age." Signature (12 years old.) 1842

49 BRITTON (J.) Celebrated author. *A N S.*

50 BRITTON (John). Author. *A N S.*

51 BRUNAULT. *D S. Vellum.* 1592

52 BUCHANAN (James). *L S.* 4to.

53 BUCKINGHAM (J. S.) *A N S. Portrait.*

54 BUEL (Judge J.) Agriculturalist. *A L S.* 4to.

55 BUGEAUD (Marshal). Duke of Issly. *A L S.* 1 p. folio.

56 BULWER (E. L.) *A L S. Initials.* 4to. 1847

57 BURDER (George). *A L S.* 1822

58 BURDER (W. V.) *A N S.*

59 BURNEY (Rev. Charles, D.D.) A Classical Scholar and Critic of high reputation. *A L S* and *A N S.*

60 BURNEY (Rev. Charles Parr, D.D.) Son of Dr. Charles Burney. *A L S.* 3 pp., 12mo.

61 BURNS (Robert). Poet. *A L.* His first sketch of a Letter of Introduction for his young friend, Mr. Wm. Duncan, to Mr. Crawford Tate. 2 pages folio. *With Portrait.* The printed copy of this letter bears the date Oct. 15, 1790.

62 BURR (Aaron). *A N.* 3d person. 1820

63 BUTTERWORTH (Joseph,) M.P. *A N S.*

64 BYRON (Lord). An interesting Letter of Inquiries, to C. B. Minagliro, relative to the Story on which his Tragedy of the "Two Foscari" was founded. Signed B. Ravenna, June 7, 1821

65 CALABRELLA (Baroness de). Novelist. *A L S.* 12mo.

66 CALANDRIN (Frances). Autograph Certificate, Identifying Jean Christophe Facio de Duillier. Also, signed by K. Burlanguy, and Jean Antoiné Gautier. Geneva, Nov. 16th, 1716. And four Autograph Envelopes. 5

67 CALHOUN (J. C.) *A L S.* 2 pp. 4to. 1825

68 CALHOUN (J. C.) *L S.* 4to.

69 CAMPBELL (Thomas). Poet. *A L S.* 12mo. *Portrait* Scarce.

70 CAMERING (C. C., M.C.) *A L S.* 4to.

71 CAREY (Mathew). *A L S.* 2 pp. 4to. 1825

72 CARLYLE (Thos.) Author. *A N S.*

73 CARNOT (L. M. N.) Minister of War under Napoleon. Eminent Mathematician. To the Duke of Plaisance. *L S. With Portrait.* Paris, May 18th, 1815

74 CARR (Sir John). English Attorney and Writer. *A L S.* 3 pp. 12mo. 1811

75 CARROL (Charles, of Carrolton.) Signer of the Declaration of Independence. Signature. Rare.

76 CARTWRIGHT (J.) Distinguished for his zealous attachment to political reform. *A N S.* 3 pp. 1811

77 CARY (H. F.) *A N S.* Feb. 2d, 1824

78 CARYNGTON (Thomas). His admission as one of the Co-brothers in the House of Friars Minors in Bedford. Original Doc. on Vellum. Very scarce, fine document. Illuminated letter. · 1479

79 CASS (Lewis). Governor of Michigan. *A L S. Portrait.* 1 pp. 8vo. 1847

80 CASS (Lewis). Circular Signed.

81 CASTELVECCHIO (Francois). *A L S.* 1 pp. French.

82 CATHERINE DE MEDICIS. *D S. On Vellum.* Poor.

83 CATINAT (Nicholas). Chief Commander of the Army of Italy. *D S. Vellum.* 1676

84 CHALMERS (Alex.) Compiler of the General Biographical Dictionary, etc. *A L S. Short Letter.*

85 CHAMBERLAIN (R.) Warrant Signed. April 20th, 1686

86 CHANNING (Wm. E.) Author. *A N S.*, and franked.

87 CHAPMAN (J. G., M.C. from Maryland.) *A L S.* 2 pp. 4to.

88 CHARLES QUINT LE GRAND, (King of France). *D S.* 1545

89 CHARLES IX. King of France, son of Catherine de Medicis. Promoter of the Massacre of St. Bartholomew. *D S. Vellum. Portrait.* Poor condition.

90 CHARLES IX., King of France. *D S. Vellum.* Very good. 1570

91 CHATEAUBRIAND. Signature.

92 CLARKE (James S., LL.D.) Domestic Chaplain to the Prince Regent. *A L S.* Dec. 27th, 1820

93 CLARKE (Mary Cowden). Authoress. *A L S.* 1 p. 4to. 1852

94 CLARKE (Mary Cowden). Authoress. *A L S.* 3 pp. 12mo

95 CLARKE (W.) Contributor to the *New Monthly*. *A L.* Initials.

96 CLAY (Henry). *A N.*, 3d person.

97 CLINTON (De Witt). Two Messages to the Legislature. Two Signatures. Jan. 6th, 1819

98 COBBETT (Wm.) *A N. Initials.*

99 COLEMAN (George). "The Younger." An Eminent Dramatist. *A N.*, 3d person. Jan. 25th, 1817

100 COLLYER (W. B.) *A L S.* Feb. 24th, 1823

101 COMBE (George). Phrenology. *A N.* 3d person. Mounted.

102 COMTE (A.) Signature and three others.

103 CONDE (Louis de Bourbon). Surnamed the Grand. *A L S.* 1 p. 4to. *Engraved Portrait.*

104 CONGREVE (Wm.) An Eminent English Dramatist. *A L S.*

105 CONSTANT (Benjamin). *A L S. With Portrait.* 1 p. 4to. 1802

106 CONSTANT (B.) French. *A N S.*

107 CONVENTION NATIONALE. An order for the arrest of "C. Citoyen Boubry," a member of the committee "de la multus Scœvola," signed by A. Dumont, Collombet, Rewbell, Mathieu Legendre and others. On the back of which is a Certificate refusing admittance to the Prison for want of room. Signed "Lavaquerié," "20th vendemiare de l'an 3e de la Republique." Folio.

108 COOKE (Eliza). Authoress of "The Old Arm Chair,"
   A L S. 2 pp. small 4to. *Portrait.*

109 COOPER (Sir Astley P.) Distinguished Surgeon. *A N.*
   3d person. 1817

110 COOPER (Dr.) *A N.*, 3d person.
   Columbia, S. C., May 25th, 1832

111 COOPER (J. Fenimore). *A S. Portrait.* 1844

112 CORE (William). Historian. *A N S.*

113 CORNWALL (Barry). *A L. Initials* B. C.

114 CORRESPONDENCE RELATIVE TO A POLITICAL INTRIGUE PLANNED BY LORD CASTLEREAGH TO ABDUCT BONAPARTE, IN 1803. Comprising 17 letters.

   It commences after the failure of the plot, and chiefly refers to pecuniary claims of the principal agents, Madame de Bonneuil and a Mr. Walter Spencer. Lord Castlereagh, in reply to Mr. Spencer's urgent appeals to relieve him and Madame de Bonneuil from their distressing situation, in consequence of liabilities incurred by them in serving government, thus coolly closes the correspondence: "Lord Castlereagh presents his Comp'ts to Mr. Spencer, and does not feel it necessary to trouble him with any observations on the letter which he received from him. London, 12 Octo." Some passages of the lady's letters are quite piquant, and remarkable for an under-current of questionable kindness toward Mr. Spencer.

115 COUTHON (George). Celebrated member of the National Convention; one of the most atrocious characters in the French Revolution; Friend of Robespierre. *A L S.* 2 pp. 4to, French, very rare.

116 COUTTS (Thomas). A London Banker, eminent for his wealth and connections. *A L S.* Short letter. 1816

117 CROKER (T. Crofton). *A L S.* 4 pp. 12mo.

118 CUNNINGHAM (Allan). *A L S.* 1 p. small 4to, very good. *Portrait. Mounted.*

119 CUSHING (Caleb). Attorney-General of the U. S., 1855. *A L S.* 1 p. 4to

120 CUSHING (Caleb). Part of *A L S*, with Signature.

121 CUSTIS (GEORGE WASHINGTON PARKE). Grand Nephew to Gen. Washington. *A Orders S.* (2). Rare.
1813

122 D'AUBIGNE (J. HENRI MERLE). Author. Guaranteed by his brother. *A L.*, signed " Henri." 8vo.
1854.

123 D'ISRAELI (I.) Author. *A L S.* 2 pp. small 4to. *Portrait.*

124 DALLAWAY (James). Author. *A L S.* Small 4to.

125 DALLAS (R.) Order signed, Nov. 24th 1820. *Mounted.*

126 DANIELL (Thomas), R.A. Author of Oriental Scenery. *A N.* 3d person.
1811

127 DEWEY (Orville). Author. *A L S.* 1 p. 4to.

128 DIBDIN (T. Coleman). *A N S.*

129 DIBBIN (T. F.) Nephew to the celebrated Song Writer. *A L S.*

130 DICK (Thomas). Author. *A L S.* 3 pp. 12mo.

131 DICKENS (Charles). *A L S.* To Charles Sumner, Esq.
1842

132 DOBBS (Arthur). Governor of North Carolina. *A L S.* 2 pp. 4to.
1757

133 DOUGLAS (George). Earl of Morton. Ticket of admission for the Bearer into the House of Lords. Sept. 6th, 1820. *Seal.*

134 DRAYTON (John). Governor of South Carolina. Signature to Proclamation. *Seal.*
1810

135 DRURY (H.) *A N S.*

136 DUDLEY (JOHN). Signature to Proclamation. Queen Anne's Reign. Proclamation for the election of delegates to the General Assembly, 1702. With the Queen's Seal. *Very rare.*

One of the First Colonial Governors of Massachusetts Bay.

137 DUVAL (Hon. G.) U. S. Senator from Florida. One of the Governors of Florida. *A L S.* 1 p. folio.   1810

138 ELLIS (HENRY). Governor of Georgia. *A L S*
4 pp. folio   Nov. 25th, 1759

Letter to the Earl of Halifax relative to resigning the Government of Georgia, etc.

139 ELLISTON (R. W.) Celebrated Actor. *A L S* Character Portrait.   Jan. 13th, 1813

140 ELTON (Chas. Abraham). Poet. Translator of Hesiod
A L S

141 EVERETT (Edward). *A L S* 4 pp., 12mo, portrait

142 FAC-SIMILE of the Act of Separation and Deed of Demission. Executed at the Meeting of the Assembly of the Free Church of Scotland, held at Edinburgh on the 23d of May, 1843

143 FAC-SIMILE of the Signatures of the Original Members of the State Society of the Cincinnati of Pennsylvania Institute   1783

144 FARADAY (Michael). An English Chemist and Natural Philosopher

145 FARIANE (Gugnon). *A L S* 4to

146 FARINGTON (Jos.), R. A. Celebrated Painter. *A L S*

147 FARQUHARSON (Capt. Gregor). Six peculiarly interesting Letters on the Repeal of the Forfeitures consequent on the Rebellions of 1715 and 1745. The Author of Junius, etc   1826

148 FAY (Theo. S.) Author. *A L S* 1p., 4to

149 FERESTI (G.) English Envoy at the Court of Ali-Pacha, 1820. *A L S* 1p., 4to   1820

150 FINDEN (Wm.) Celebrated English Engraver. *A N S*

151 FLINT (Sir Chas.) *A N* 3d person. Irish Office   1822

152 FOUQUIER (A. Q.) Order signed for the Arrest of 44 persons. With seal   1793

153 FRAGMENTS Traduit du 4e Livre de l'Eneide, par M. Sallion de Nantes

154 FRANCIS I., KING OF FRANCE. Signature good, but document has been scorched. *D S Vellum.* 1529

155 FRANCIS I. Second Year of his Reign. Good. *D S Vellum.* Portrait   1516

156 FRANKLIN (BENJAMIN). *A L S* 4to, 2pp   1783

Letter relating to the terms on which lands may be acquired in America, and the manner of beginning new Settlements on them.

157 FREDERICK THE GREAT, King of Prussia. *L S* 4to, Potsdam, Oct. 12th, 1777

158 FREELING (J. C.) *A N* 3d person   1819

159 FRY (Elizabeth). Philanthropist. *A L S*   1821

160 FULLER (S. Margaret). Authoress   *A N S*

161 GAGE (GEN. THOMAS). British General. To Col. Bradstreet. *A L S* 1 p., 4to. June 10th, 1765.

162 GALES (Joseph). Editor National Intelligencer. Washington, D. C   *A L S*

163 GARRICK (David). Actor. *A L S* 4 pp, 12mo, *very rare*   1774

164 GARRICK, Grimaldi, Kemble, Siddons, etc. *A E* 8

165 GEORGE II., King of Great Britain. Doc. S. *Vellum*
1765

    Appointing Thomas Lloyd Lieut. of the Independent Company of Foot in Province of So. Ca.

166 GEORGE III., King of Great Britain. *When Blind.* *D S* With Seal

167 GEORGE III., King of Great Britain. *D S* 2 pp, folio. Portrait. Fine

168 GILMAN (Caroline). *A L S* 1 p, 4to

169 GODOLPHIN (Sidney, Earl of). Lord High Treasurer. *D S* Portrait

170 GODWIN (William). *A L S* 2 pp, small 4to

171 GOLDSMITH (Lewis). Celebrated Jew. *A L S*

    This Letter is to Mr. Colburn, who, in his Dictionary of Living Authors, speaks unfavorably of his Works. The last of the letter runs thus: "I did not expect that you would have been the medium through which my character has been libelled, and I shall certainly not let the matter rest where it does."

172 GREENWOOD (Grace). [Sara J. Clarke.] Authoress and Poetess. *A L S* Small 4to

ACKETT (Maria). Authoress. *A L S*

174 HALIBURTON (Judge). Sam Slick. *A N* 3d person

175 HALL (Mrs. S. C.) Authoress. *A N* 3d person. Portrait *Mounted*

176 HAMILTON (Alex.) Signature

177 HANRIOT (Françoise). Order signed "Hanriot."

    An Order to keep "le Citoyen, Montalant Adjutant General 6th Legion," in solitary confinement.

178 HARCOURT (Lord). And four others. *A E*

179 HASLEWOOD (J.) *A L S* 4to

180 HEATH (T.) Engraver. *A L S*   1810

181 HENRY II., King of France. *D S*   *Vellum.*   Good order   1594

182 HENRY III., King of France. *D S*   *Vellum*

183 HENRY III. *D S*   1574

184 HENRY IV., King of France and Navarre, surnamed the Great. Assassinated in 1610. *D S*   *On parchment, poor*

185 HENRY IV. *D S*   *Vellum, good*   1540

186 HENRY IV. *L S* 4to. Has been mended on parchment.

187 HENRY (Patrick). Signature

188 HERBERT (Henry Wm.) Frank Forrester. *A L S* 2 pp, 12mo

189 HERVEY (Sir Wm.) Ministre Françoise. Passport signed Paris, 1847

190 HERSCHEL (SIR JOHN F. W.) A TREATISE ON ASTRONOMY. *Proof corrected by the author.* Contains many additions in the author's autograph. Folio, *cloth, not complete*

191 HERVI (Peter). Author. *A L S*   1824

192 HIPPISLEY (J. Hunt). Author.   *A N S*

193 HOARE (Prince.) Dramatic Author. *A L S* 2 pp, 12mo.

194 HOFFMAN (C. F.) Author. *A N S* 2 pp.

195 HOLDERNESS (Mary). *A L S*

195*HOLROYD (John Baker). Lord Sheffield. *A N* 3d person *Mounted*

196 HONE (Wm.) Author. *A L S* 3 pp, small 4to

197 HOOK (Theodore E.) Celebrated Novelist and Dramatic Writer *A L S*

198 HOPITAL (Michael de l'). Eminent Chancellor of France. *D S Parchment*

199 HOWE (S. G.) Author. *A L S* 2 pp, 4to

200 HOWITT (Mary). *A N S* 2 pp, 12mo. *Portrait*

201 HOWITT (Wm.) Author. *A L S* 4 pp, 12mo, *very good*

202 HOWLEY (Right Rev. William). Lord Bishop of London. *A L S* 12mo, 4pp. Signed W. London

203 HUGHES (James). To W. Blair. *A L S* 1813

204 HUGO (Victor). *A N S*

205 HUMBOLDT (ALEXANDER VON). Philosopher and Traveller. *A L S* French, very neat specimen. Dated from L'Ecole Polyt.

206 HUMBOLDT (ALEX. VON). *A N S*

207 HUME (Joseph), M.P. *A L S* 2 pp, 12mo 1823

208 HUSKISSON (Right Hon. Wm.) An English Statesman. *A N* 3d person. Nov. 2d, 1817

209 HUTCHINSON (THOMAS). Governor of Massachusetts. Bill S. *Very rare* 1751

210 HUTTON (Catherine). Authoress and Autograph Collector. *A L S* Feb. 20th, 1823

211 HUTTON (Chas.) LL.D. Eminent Mathematician. *A L S* Dec. 15th, 1821

NGERSOLL (C. J.) *A N S*

213 IRELAND (Wm. Henry). HAMLET. Autograph manuscript, folio, *half russia*

> A correct transcript of the First, Second and Fourth Acts, and half of the 1st Scene of the Fifth Act.
>
> "Mr. Samuel Ireland's enthusiastic admiration of the Works of Shakespeare being his general theme of conversation, that circumstance prompted his son, William Henry, to imbibe a similar sentiment. In consequence of such predilections, the latter had undertaken to copy out all the dramas of the Immortal Bard: which labor he commenced with the present fair specimen of Hamlet. The undertaking, however, thus begun, was put a stop to by the production of the spurious papers, attributed, by W. H. Ireland, to Shakespeare. So that the present volume is particularly curious, as having been the labor of the writer immediately prior to the celebrated fabrication which so long occupied the attention of the literary world."

214 IRVING (Washington). Fac-Simile. *A L S* 3 pp. *With portrait* 1852

215 IRVING (W.) *A L* Initials. *Portrait*

216 IRVING (Washington.) *A N*

217 ISOGRAPHIE DES HOMMES CELEBRES ou Collection de Fac-Similes de Lettres Autographes et de Signatures. Executée et Imprimée par Th. Delarue, Lithographe. 4 vols. 4to, *half morocco* Paris, 1843

> An exceedingly valuable collection, and indispensable to an Autograph Collector.

JACKSON (John). Eminent Portrait Painter. *A N S*

219 JAMESON (Anna). *A N S*

220 JENCKINSON (Robert Banks). Lord Hawkesbury. *A N*

221 JEFFERSON (Thos.) Letter Relating to a Collection of the Laws of America, some of which he believed to be the only Copies in existence. *A L S* 2 pp, 4to, *good, but torn* 1805

222 JEFFERSON (Thos.) President of the United States, to the Governor of Rhode Island. *L S* 4to *Portrait* 1791

223 JEFFREY (Francis). Editor of Edinburgh Review. *A L S*
4to, *rare*

224 JOHNSON (Richard M.) Governor of Kentucky. Colonel in the War 1812. The man that is said "To have killed Tecumseh." *A N* 3d person. 4to

225 JOHNSON (Sir Wm.) Commander in America, 1755. *A L S* 1 p, folio

226 JOSEPH, KING OF SPAIN. *A L S*

227 JOSEPHINE, EMPRESS OF FRANCE. Letter signed 4to, *with portrait*

228 KELLERMAN (F. E.) Duke of Valmy; one of the greatest Generals of the Empire. *A L S* 3 pp, 12mo

229 KEMPE (Mrs.) Mother of Mrs. Chas. Stothard. *A N* 3d person. 4 pp 1821

230 KENYON (George). Lord Kenyon. *A N* 3d person 1819

231 KIRKLAND (Mrs. C. M.) Authoress. *A L S* 1 p

232 KITCHENER (Wm.) Physician and Miscellaneous Writer. *A L S*

233 LAFAYETTE (GEN.) *A L S* French. *Portrait* 1828

234 LALLY (THOMAS ARTHUR) COUNT. An Irish Officer attached to the House of Stuart, and in the Service of France. Was beheaded in 1766. *A L S* 2 pp, 4to. French April 15th, 1757

235 LAMB (LADY CAROLINE). *A N* 3d person

236 LANDMANN (Geo.) Author. *A N S*

237 LANDSEER, Cooper, Constable, etc   A E 66

238 LANGLAL (L.)   French.   A L S

239 LANMAN (Charles).   A L S and six others.

240 LATROBE (H.)   Architect.   A N S

241 LAWRENCE (Abbot).   U. S. Minister to England.   A L S
    1 p, 4to   1843

242 LAWRENCE (SIR THOMAS).   Celebrated Painter.
    A L S.   1809

243 LEE (John).   Celebrated Traveller.   A L S.   1 p. 4to.

244 LEGARÉ (H. S.)   M. C.   A L S.   2 pp. folio.

245 LEGENDRE (Louis).   French Revolutionist, surnamed the
    Butcher.   D S.   With 15 other Autographs on the
    Document, being Members of the Committee of Public
    Safety, including Merlin de Douay, Lacombe, La Porte,
    etc.

245*LEHOTE (Agnes M.)   A L S.   1836

246 LINDLEY (Dr. John).   Botanist.   A N.

247 LORRAINE (Charles de), duc de Mayenne.   D S.   Vellum

248 LORUE (Petit de la).   A L S.   1 pp. French.

249 LOUDON (J. C.)   Horticulturist.   A L S. 12mo.   1840

250 LOUIS XII. (KING OF FRANCE).   D S on vellum.
    Fine specimen, very rare   1504

251 LOUIS XIV. (KING OF FRANCE AND NAVAR-
    RE).   D S.   Vellum, poor   1610

252 LOUIS XIV. (KING OF FRANCE AND NAVAR-
    RE).   D S.   Vellum, good.   1666

253 LOUIS XV. (KING OF FRANCE AND NAVAR-
    RE)..   D S vellum, very fine.   July 29th, 1761

254 LOUIS XVI. (KING OF FRANCE). Guillotined Jan.
21st, 1793. *D S.* 1 p. folio   1788

255 LOWE (Sir Hudson). Governor of St. Helena, while that Island was the place of detention of the Emperor Napoleon. *A N.*, 3d person.   1822

256 LOWRY (Wilson), F.R.S. Eminent Engraver. *A N S* 3d person.

257 LYELL (Charles). Geologist. *A N S.* 2 pp. 12mo

258 LYSANS (Rev. Daniel). Magna Britannica. *A N.*, 3d person

259 McDONALD (MOSES). M. C. from Maine. *A L S.* 4to.   1854

260 McLANE (John). Postmaster-General. *L S. Portrait.* Repaired.

261 McLANE (Lewis). Ex-Minister to England. *A L S.* 3 pp. 12mo.

262 MACDONALD (Marshal). *A L S.* 2 pp. 4to. *Portrait.*   1828

263 MACGREGOR (J.) Author. *L S.* Folio.

264 MACKENZIE (William). *A L S.*   1844

265 MACKINTOSH (Sir James). Life of Sir Thomas More, original manuscript in the Author's Autograph, with corrections, etc. 4to, *half calf.* Not complete.

266 MACOMBE (A. C.) Circular signed.   1826

267 MAITLAND (James). Earl of Lauderdale, K.T. *A L S.* 7 pp. 12mo.   1822

268 MAJENDI (Henry William). Bishop of Bangor. *A E. Mounted.*

269 MALTBY (E.) Bishop of Chichester. *A L S.* Signed E. Chichester. Small 4to. 1836

270 MARGUERITE (QUEEN OF FRANCE AND NAVARRE). *D S. Vellum.*

271 MARMONT (AUG. F. L. VIESSE). Marshal of France. *A L S.*, 4to, with an engraving. *Scarce.* Good.

272 MASSENA (ANDRÉ). Marshal of France. *L S.* With *Portrait. Scarce.* 1815

273 MATHEWS (Cornelius). "Big Abel." *A N S.* 1843

274 MATHEWS (C.) Comedian. *A N S.*

275 MAZZINI (Guiseppe). Italian Patriot, whose letters were opened by the English Government. *A N S.*

276 MERCER (C. F.) Judge of Superior Court. *A L S.* 3 pp. 4to. 1835

277 MEYRICK (Sir Samuel). Author of "Arms and Armour," *A L S.* 1 pp. 12mo.

278 MILLS (Charles). Historian. *A N S.*

279 MITCHELL (T.) Translator of Aristophanes. *A L S.*

280 MITFORD (Miss Mary Russell). Authoress. *A L S.* 1 p. 4to. *Portrait.*

281 MONNEY (William). Author. *A N.*, 3d person. June 7th, 1816

282 MONROE (JAMES). President. *A N.*, 3d person.

283 MONTAGU (Basil), of Lincoln's Inn. Author. *A L S.*

284 MONTAGU (Lady Mary). *A N.*, 3d person.

285 MONTGOMERY (J.) Distinguished Irish and English Poet. *A L S.* 1858

286 MONTRAY (J.) *A N S.* 1822

287 MORGAN (Lady Sidney). Authoress, France, Italy, etc. *A L S.* 2 pp. 12mo. *Portrait.*

288 MORGAN (Lady). Novelist. *A N S.*

289 MORIER (James). Author. *A N.*

290 MORNAY (PHILIP DE). Celebrated French Statesman and Writer. *D S.* On parchment. With *Portrait.*

291 MORRIS (Commodore Jacob). U. S. Navy. *L S.*, 4to.

292 MORTON (Dr. W. T. G.) Discoverer of the application of Ether. *A L S.* 12mo.

293 MUDFORD (Wm.) Author. *A L S.* 3 pp. 16mo.

294 MURCHISON (Sir Roderick). Author. *A N S.*

295 MURRAY (William). Third Earl of Mansfield. Autograph Ticket for Admission to the Bearer, below the Bar. Signed, Mansfield. *Seal.*

296 NARES (ROBERT). Philologist. *A L S.*

297 NELSON, HORATIO, (Viscount, Duke of Bronte). *L S.* Folio.
Albemarle, Woolwich, Sept. 8th, 1781

298 NELSON (Hon. John). New York. *A L S.* 2 pp. 4to. 1822

299 NEVILLE (Richard Aldworth). Lord Braybrooke, LL.D. *A N.*, 3d person. 1822

300 NEY (MICHAEL). Marshal of France. *D S. Fine specimen and rare.* Signed as Commander-in-Chief of the army intended to invade England. To General Dutailles.

301 NICHOLSON (Commodore Wm. B.) Naval Commissioner
L S. 1 p. 4to.

302 NORTHCOTE (JAMES), R.A. Eminent Portrait and Historical Painter, and Author. A L S.. 1812

303 NORTHUMBERLAND (Algernon Percy, Earl of.) D S. Signed also by Pembroke, Sir H. Vane, Henry Mildmay and James Bond. 1647

304 NOURSE (Joseph). U. S. Treasurer. A O S. 1810

305 ONSLOW (Arthur). Speaker for the House of Commons.
D S April 18th, 1745

306 OPIE (Amelia). Distinguished Authoress. Born 1771.
A L S 3 pp, 12mo 1823

307 ORIGINAL LETTERS COLLECTED BY WILLIAM UPCOTT OF THE LONDON INSTITUTION, Containing Two Thousand and Sixty-nine Original Letters and Autographs. Illustrated with three hundred and thirty-one portraits—the whole of an octavo size—comprising celebrated and remarkable persons in all stations of life; such as the family of George III., Peers, Bishops, Baronets, Naval and Military Characters, and Literary Men, including Poets, and Dramatic Writers, Travellers, Painters, Sculptors, Architects and Engravers; Actors, Composers, Clerical, Legal, Medical and Public Characters; Men of Science, Eminent Women and distinguished Foreigners. Bound in 31 vols., 8vo, *half russia calf*, forming one of the most complete and valuable collections of Autographs ever offered to the public. Mr. Upcott considered it the gem of his extensive collection, and refused £300 for the set. When the contents of the volumes are examined, they cannot fail to create a peculiar interest, embodying as they do many of the most remarkable persons. The Contents of the volumes are as follows:

ABBREVIATIONS.

A. Autograph Letter or Note not Signed.
S. Signature only.
D. S. Document Signed.
L. S. Letter (in other writing) Signed.

Articles to which no abbreviations are attached are entirely Autographic and Signed.

VOLUME I.

Regal

George the Third. Portrait, *s*.
George the Fourth. do. *s*.
Frederick, Duke of York. Portrait, *a*.
—— do. Frank.
William Henry, Duke of Clarence.
—— Portrait.
—— Frank.
—— Frank.
Edward, Duke of Kent. Portrait.
—— Frank.
Augustus Frederick, Duke of Sussex.
Portrait. *a*.
—— Frank.
Adolphus Fred'k, Duke of Cambridge.
Portrait, *s*.
William Frederick, Duke of Gloucester.
—— Frank.
—— do.

Archiepiscopal.

Charles Manners Sutton, Canterbury.
Edward Venables Vernon, York. Port.

Ducal.

Argyll, George William Campbell. *a*.
Atholl, John.
Beaufort, Henry Charles Somerset.
—— William George Henry Somerset (Rev.)
—— Brother of the Duke.
Bedford, John Russell.
—— do.
—— Francis, Marquess of Tavistock. Eldest son.
—— George William Russell. *a*.
Buckingham, Richard Grenville Chandos Temple.
—— when Marquess. *a*.
—— as Duke. *a*.
—— Richard Plantagenet, Marquess of Chandos. Eldest son.
Devonshire, Wm. Spencer Cavendish. *a*.
—— do.
—— Georgiana, Duchess. Portrait.
—— Elizabeth Foster, pres. Duchess.
—— Lady Cavendish. *a*.

Dorset, Charles Sackville.
—— do.
—— Arabella Diana Cope. Third Duchess.
Gordon, Alexander Gordon.
—— do. *a*.
—— do.
—— do.
Grafton, George Henry Fitzroy.
—— Lord William Fitzroy, brother to the Duke.
—— Lord John Fitzroy.
Hamilton & Brandon, Alexander, as M. of Douglas and Clydesdale.
—— as Duke.
—— as Duke. *a*.
Leeds, George William Frederick Osborne. Frank.
Leinster, Augustus Fred'k Fitzgerald.
Manchester, William Montagu. *a*.
Marlborough, Geo. Spencer Churchill.
—— do.
—— George, Marquess of Blandford.
Montrose, James Graham.
Newcastle, Henry Pelham Clinton.
Norfolk, Charles. Eleventh Duke. *a*.
—— Bernard Edward Howard. Twelfth and present Duke.
Northumberland, Hugh Percy.
—— Charlotte, Duchess. *a*.
Portland, William Henry Bentinck. *a*.
—— Wm. Henry Cavendish Scott Bentinck. The pres. Duke.
—— do.
—— Lord Wm., Hon. Cavendish Bentinck. Next brother to the Duke.
—— Lord Charles Bentinck.
Richmond, Chas. Lennox. Pres. Duke.
Roxburghe, John Norcliffe Innes Ker.
Rutland, John Henry Manners. *a*.
—— do. *a*.
—— do.
—— do.
St. Albans, William Beauclerk.
—— Maria Janetta, Duchess.
Somerset, Edward Adolphus Seymour.
—— do. *a*.

Wellington, Arthur Wellesley. Port.

VOLUME II.

Marquesses.

Downshire, Arthur Blundell S. T. Hill. Third Marquess.
—— as Earl of Hillsborough.
Abercorn, John James Hamilton. First Marquess.
—— Anne Jane, Marchioness.
Ailesbury, Charles Bruce. First Marquis. *a.*
—— Anne Elizabeth, his Mother.
Anglesey, Henry Wm. Paget. First Marquess. Portrait.
Bath, Thos. Thynne. Second Marquess.
—— Isabella Bying. Marchioness.
—— Lord John Thynne.
Bute, John Critchon Stuart. Second Marquess.
—— do. Frank.
Cambden, Lord Jeffries Pratt. First Marquess. *a.*
Cholmondley, George James. First Marquess.
Conyngham, Henry. First Marquess.
——Elizab'h Denison. Marchioness. *a*
—— Lord Francis Conyngham. *a.*
Donegall, George Augustus Chichester. Second Marquess. Frank.
—— as Baron Fisherwick.
—— Anna May. Marchioness. *a.*
—— George Hamilton. Earl of Belfast.
Ely, John Loftus. Second Marquess.
—— do. *a.*
Exeter, Brownlow Cecil. Second Marquess.
Hastings, Francis Raudon. First Marquis. Portrait.
Headfort, Thomas Taylour. Second Earl, and First Marquess.
—— Mary Quin. Marchioness. *a.*
—— Thomas. Earl of Bective. *a.*
Hertford, Francis Ingram Seymour Conway. First Marquess.

Herford, Francis Chas. Second Marq.
—— do. Frank.
—— do. when Lord Yarmouth.
Huntley, George. Marquess. Frank.
Landsdowne, Henry Petty. Third Marquess.
Londonderry, Charles Wm. Vane Stewart. Third Marquess. Frank.
Lothian, John Kerr. Seventh Marquess.
Northampton, Charles Compton. First Marquess. *a.*
—— Margaret Clepham, Lady Compton. *a.*
Queenberry, Chas. Douglass. Marquess.
Salisbury, Jas. Cecil. First Marquess.*a.*
Sligo, Howe, Peter Browne. Second Marquess.
—— do. *a.*
—— Lady Louisa Catherine Howe. First Marchioness. *a.*
Stafford, George Granville Levison Gower. Second Marquess.
—— Elizabeth, Countess of Sutherland. Marchioness. *a.*
Thomond, William O'Brien. Second Marquess.
Townshend, George. Second Marquess.
Tweeddale, George Hay. Eighth Marquis. Frank.
Waterford, Henry de la Poer Beresford. Second Marquess.
Wellesley, Richard. First Marquess. Portrait.
Winchester, Charles Ingoldsby Paulet. Thirteenth Marquess.

Earls.

Aberdeen, George Hamilton Gordon. Fourth Earl. *a.*
Abergavenny, Henry Neville. Second Earl.
Abingdon, Montague Bertie. Fifth Earl.
—— Emily Gage, his Countess. *a.*
Aboyne, George Gordon. Fifth Earl. Signed Meldrum.
—— do. Frank.

Albermarle, William Charles Keppel. Fourth Earl.
Ashburnham, George. Third Earl.
——— Sophia Thynne, his wife. *a.*
Balcarras, Alexander Lindsay. Sixth Earl.
Bandon, Francis Bernard. First Earl. Frank.
Bathurst, Henry. Third Earl. *a.*
Beauchamp, William B. Lygon. Second Earl.
——— Lady Charlotte Pindar. *a.*
Belmore, Somerset Lowry Corrie. Second Earl. *a.*
Bessborough, Frederick Ponsonby. Third Earl. *a.*
——— do.
Blessington, Charles John Gardiner.
——— do.
——— as Mountjoy.
Bradford, George Bridgman. Second Earl.
Breadalbane, John Campbell. Fourth Earl.
Bridgewater, John William Egerton. Seventh Earl.
——— do. *a.*
——— do.
Bristol, Frederick William Hervey. Fifth Earl.
——— do. *a.*
Brownlow, John Cust. First Earl.
——— do.
Buckinghamshire, George Robert Hobart. Fifth Earl.

———

VOLUME III.

Caledon, Dupré, Alex'r. Second Earl
Cardigan, Robt. Brudenell. Sixth Earl.
Carlisle, Frederick Howard. Fifth Earl. Portrait. *a.*
Carnavon, Henry George Herbert. Second Earl.
Carrick, Somerset, Richard Butler. Third Earl. Frank.

Carysford, John Joshua Proby. First Earl.
——— do.
Cassilis, Archibald Kennedy. Twelfth Earl.
Cathcart, William Shaw. First Earl. Portrait—Frank.
Charlemont, Francis William Caulfield. Second Earl. Frank.
Charleville, Charles William Bury First Earl. Frank.
——— Catherine Maria D. Countess. *a.*
Chatham, John Pitt. Second Earl.
Chesterfield, Philip Stanhope. Fifth Earl. Frank.
Chichester, Thomas Pelham. Second Earl. *a.*
Clancarty, Richard Le Poer French. First Earl. Frank.
——— Henrietta Margaret Staples. Countess. *a.*
Clare, John Fitzgibbon. Second Earl. *a.*
Clarendon, Thos. Villiers. Sec'd Earl.
——— do.
Cork, Edmund Boyle. Eighth Earl.
——— do. Frank.
——— Lord Boyle.
Cornwallis, Charles. Second Marquess and third Earl.
Cornwallis, James Mann. Fifth Earl. Frank.
Coventry, George Wm. Seventh Ear'.
——— George William. Viscount Deerhurst.
Courtown, James Stopford. Second Earl. Signed " Sallerford."
Cowper, Peter Leopold Cowper. Fifth Earl. *a.*
Craven, William Craven. First Earl.
Dalhousie, George Ramsay. Ninth Earl. Frank.
Darlington, William Henry Vane. Third Earl.
Darnley, John Bligh. Fourth Earl. *a.*
Dartmouth, George Legge. Third Earl. *a.*
——— Edward, Lord Clifton.
——— do.

De Grey, Amable Hume Campbell. Baroness Lucas, and first Countess.
———— do.
———— do. *a.*
De La Warr, George John West. Fifth Earl. *a.*
Denbigh, Wm. Fielding. Seventh Earl.
Derby, Edward Smith Stanley. Twelfth Earl. *a.*
———— Edward, Lord Stanley.
Donoughmore, Richard Hely Hutchinson. First Earl. Portrait. *a.*
Egmont, John James Perceval. Third Earl. Frank.
Egremont, George Wyndham. Third Earl.
Eldon, John Scott. First Earl. Port.
Enneskillen, John Willoughby Cole. Second Earl.
Erne, John Creighton. First Earl.
———— Lady Mary Caroline Hervey. Countess.
Errol, William George Henry Carr. Sixteenth Earl.
Essex, George Capel. Fifth Earl.
———— do.
———— do.
———— do.
Falmouth, Edw. Boscawen. First Earl.
Farnham, John James Barry. Second Earl.
———— Grace Cuff, his lady. *a.*
Ferrers, Robert Shirley. Seventh Earl.
Fitzwilliam, Robert Wentworth. Fourth Earl.
Fortescue, Hugh. First Earl.
———— Hugh Viscount Ebrington.
Galloway, Geo. Stewart. Eighth Earl.
———— do.
———— also, signed "Stewart of Gerties."
Glasgow, George Boyle. Fourth Earl. Frank. Signed "Ross."
Gosford, Archibald Atcheson. Second Earl.
Gower, George Granville Leveson. Earl. *a.* (Duke of Sutherland.)
Grey, Charles. Second Earl.
Grosvenor, Robert. Second Earl. Port.
Guilford, Frederick North. Fifth Earl.

Guilford, Susan Coutts, wife of George North, third Earl. *a.*
———— do.
———— do.

VOLUME IV.

Harborough, Philip Sherard. Frank.
Harcourt, George Simon. *a.*
Harcourt, William. Third Earl. Frank.
———— do. do.
Hardwicke, Philip York. Third Earl.
———— do. *a.*
Harewood, Henry Lascelles. Second Earl.
Harrington, Charles Stanhope. Third Earl. Portrait.
———— Jane Fleming, his Countess.
Harrowby, Dudley Ryder. First Earl.
———— Hon. F. D. Ryder.
Home, Alexander Ramsay. Tenth Earl.
Hopetown, John. Baron Niddry. Fourth Earl.
Howe, Asheton Curzon. Visct. Curzon.
Huntington, Hans Francis Hastings. Twenty-eighth Earl.
Ilchester, Henry Strangeways. Third Earl.
Jersey, George Villiers. Fifth Earl.
———— Lady Sarah Fane, his lady. *a.*
———— do. *a.*
Kellie, Thomas Erskine. Earl. Frank.
Kingsborough, Viscount.
———— George King. Earl. Father of the preceding.
Lauderdale, James Maitland. Eighth Earl.
———— do.
———— do. *l. s.*
———— do. *l. s.*
Leicester, George Thousand. Twentieth Earl. *a.*
Leitrim, Nath. Clements. Second Earl.
———— Mary Birmingham, his lady. *a.*
Limerick, Edmund Henry Percy. First Earl. *a.*
———— do.
Liverpool, Robert Banks Jenkinson. Portrait.
Loven, Alex'r Melville. Seventh Earl.

Longford, Thos. Pakenham. First Earl.
—— do.
Lucan, Rich'd Bingham. Second Earl.
—— Margaret Smith, wife of Chas. Bingham, first Earl.
Lonsdale, William Lowther. Second Earl. *a.*
Macclesfield, Geo. Parker. Fourth Earl.
Malmesbury, James Edward Harris. Second Earl.
—— Harriet Mary Amyand, wife of James, first Earl. *a.*
Maysfield, David Murray. Second Earl.
Mansfield, Wm. Murray. Third Earl.
Manvers, Chas. Pierrepont. First Earl.
Mayo, John Bourke. Fourth Earl.
Minto, Gilbert Elliott. Second Earl.
{ Morley, John Parker. Sixteenth Earl, and first Baron Douglass of Loch Leven. } *Error.*
Morley, John Parker. Viscount Barrington, and first Earl Morley.
—— do.
Morton, George. Sixteenth Earl, and first Baron Douglass of Loch Leven. *a.*
—— do. *a.*
—— Countess Morton. *a.*
Moray, Francis Stuart. Ninth Earl, and Baron Stuart, of Castle Stuart.
Mount Cashel, Stephen Moore. Second Earl.
Mount Edgcumb, Rich'd. Second Earl.
Mulgrave, Edmund Sheffield. Fourth Earl.
Mount Norris, Arthur Annesley. First Earl.
Nelson & Bronte, Rev. William, D.D. First Earl.
O'Neill, Charles St. John. First Earl.
Onslow, Thomas. Second Earl.
Orford, Horatio Walpole. Sixth Earl.
Ormonde, James Butler. Nineteenth Earl of the second Marquess, and Baron Butler.
—— James Butler, M.P. One of younger sons of the preceding.
Oxford, Edward Harley. Fifth Earl.

Pembroke and Montgomery, George Augustus. First Earl.
Plymouth, Other Arthur Windsor. Sixth Earl.
Pomfret, George Fermor. Third Earl.
Portsmouth, John Charles Wallup. *a.*
Poulett, John. Fifth Earl. Frank.
Powis, Edward Clive. Sixth Earl. *a.* Third Earl.
—— Henrietta Antonia, Lady Powis. *a.*
—— Robert Clive.

VOLUME V.

Radnor, Jacob Bouverie. Second Earl.
—— Wm. P. Bouverie. Viscount Folkestone. *a.*
Rockford, William Henry Nassau. Fifth Earl. Frank.
Rocksavage, Earl of. Frank.
Roden, Robert. Third Earl. Frank.
Romney, Chas. Marshen. Second Earl.
Rosse, Laurence Parsons. Second Earl.
—— William, Lord Oxmantown, his son, now Lord Ross.
Roseberry, Archibald John Primrose. Fourth Earl.
Rosslyn, Sir James Sinclair Erskine. Second Earl.
St. Helens, Alleyne Fitz Herbert.
St. Vincent, Sir John Jervis. First Earl. Portrait.
Sandwich, John Montagu. Fifth Earl. *a.*
—— Lord Hinchinbroke.
Scarborough, George Lumley Sanderson. Fifth Earl. *a.*
Selkirk, Dunbar, James Douglas. Sixth Earl. *a.*
Shaftesbury, Cropley Ashley Cooper. Sixth Earl.
Shannon, Henry Boyle. Earl of Shannon, and Baron Castleton.
Sheffield, John Baker Holroyd. First Earl. *a.* Portrait.
Somers, J. Somers Cocks. First Earl. *a.*
—— Anne, Dowager Countess. *a.*

Spencer, George John. Second Earl Portrait. *a.*
Stamford and Warrington, George Harry. Sixth Earl.
Stanhope, Charles. Third Earl. Frank.
―― Philip Henry. Fourth Earl. *a.*
Stradbroke, John. Second Earl.
Suffolk and Berkshire, Thomas Howard. Sixteenth Earl.
―― Lord Henry Howard. *a.*
Talbot, Chas. Chetwynd. Third Earl.
Thanet, Sackville Tufton. Ninth Earl.
Verulam, Jas. Grimston. First Earl. *a.*
Waldegrave, John James. Sixth Earl.
Warwick, George Greville. Thirtieth Earl.
―― Countess Warwick. *a.*
Westmoreland, John Fane. Tenth Earl. *a.*
Whitworth, Lord.
Wicklow, Wm. Howard. Third Earl.
Wilton, Thos. Egerton. Second Earl.
Winchelsea, George French Hatton. Ninth Earl.

Viscounts.

Anson, Thomas. First Viscount. *a.*
―― Thomas William. Now Earl of Litchfield.
―― Ann M. Cooke Viscountess, wife Lord Thomas. *a.*
Anson, Ann M. Cook.
―― do. *a. Error.*
Arbuthnot, John Eighth Viscount. *a.*
Beresford, William Carr. First Viscount. Frank.
Bolingbroke, Henry St. John. Fourth Viscount.
Carleton, Henry. Viscount Boyle, and Baron Carleton.
Clifton, Henry Agar Ellis.
Downe, John B. C. Dawney. Fifth Viscount.
Dudley and Ward, William. Third Viscount.
Duncan, Robert. Second Viscount.
Exmouth, Sir Edward Pettew. First Viscount.
Gage, Henry Hall.

Gore, Chas. Vercher. Second Viscount.
Granville, Granville Levison Gower. First Viscount.
Hampden, Thomas Trevor.
Hereford, Henry Devereux. Fourteenth Viscount.
―― Lady Hereford, his wife. *a.*
Hood, Henry. Second Viscount.
Lake, Francis Gerard. Second Viscount. Portrait.
Lorton, Robert Edward King. First Viscount.
Maynard, Henry. Third Viscount.
Melbourne, Wm. Lamb. Second Visc't.
Melville, Robert Saunders Dundas. Second Viscount.
Middleton, George Brodrick. Fourth Viscount.
Sidmouth, Henry Addington. First Viscount. Portrait.
―― Lady Sidmouth, his wife. *a.*
Sydney, John Robert Townshend. Third Viscount.
Templetown, John Henry. *a.*
―― Eliz. Boughton. Lady Dowager. *a.*
Torrington, George Bying. Sixth Viscount.

―――

VOLUME VI.

Episcopal.

Bangor—John Randolph, D.D.
    Henry William Majendié.
Bath and Wells—Richard Beadon! *a.*
    do. *l. s.*
    John Henry Law. *a.*
Bristol—William Love Mansel. *a.*
    do.
    John Kaye.
Carlisle—Samuel Goodenough. *a.*
Chester—George Henry Law.
    Charles James Bloomfield.
Chichester—John Buckner.
Cork—Honorable Thomas Laurence.
Down and Connor—Richard Mant.
Dublin—William

Durham—Hon. Shute Barrington. *a.*
                        Portrait.
          do.   Frank.
Ely—Bowyer Edward Sparke.
Exeter—Hon. George Pelham.
          William Carey.
Gloucester—Wm. Warburton. Port.
          Hon. Henry Ryder. do.
Hereford—Geo. Isaac Huntingford. *a.*
Llandaff—Richard Watson. Portrait.
          William Van Mildart. *a.*
          do.   Frank.
Litchfield ⎧ Richard Hurd.
and   ⎨ Hon. James Cornwallis.
Coventry   ⎩ Hon. Henry Ryder. Frank.
Limerick—John Webb. *a.*
Lincoln—George Prettyman Tomline.
          Hon. George Pelham. *a.*
London—Beilby Porteus. Portrait. *a.*
          William Howley.
          do.
Norwich—Henry Bathurst. Portrait.
Oxford—Hon. Edward Legge.
Peterborough—Herbert Marsh.
                        do.
Rochester—Walker King.
St. Asaph—Samuel Horsley. Portrait.
          William Cleaver.
          John Luxmore.
St. Davids—Thomas Burgess. Frank.
Sarum—John Fisher.
          do.   *a.*
Tuam—Hon. Power Le Poer French.
Winchester—Geo. Prettyman Tomline.
          do.
Worcester—Richard Hurd. Portrait.
          Foliot Herbert Walker
            Cornwall.
                        do.

VOLUME VII.
Barons.

Abercromby, George. Second Baron. Frank.
Alvanley, Wm. Arden. Second Baron.
Amherst, Wm. Pitt. Second Baron. *a.*
Arden, Charles George Percival. First Baron. Frank.
———   do.

Arundell, Jas. Everard. Tenth Baron.
Auckland William Eden. First Baron.
——— George Eden. Second Baron. *a.*
Audley, George Thicknesse Touchet. Nineteenth Baron.
Bagot, William. Second Baron.
Barham, Chas. Middleton. First Baron.
Barrymore, Richard Barry. *a.*
Bayning, Charles Fred. Powlett. Second Baron.
Belhaven and Stenton, Robert Hamilton. Eighth Baron.
Berwick, Thomas Noel Hill. Second Baron.
Bexley, Nicholas Vansittart. First Baron. *a.*
Bolton, William Orde Powlett. Second Baron.
Braybrook, Richard Aldworth Neville.
Buchan, David Stuart Erskine. Sixth Baron.
Bulkeley, Thomas James.
Byron, George Anson. Seventh Baron.
Calthorpe, Geo. Gough. Third Baron. *a.*
———   do.   Frank.
Carrington, Robert Smith.
Carteret, George Thynne. Second Baron. Frank.
Cawdor, John Frederick Campbell. Second Baron. *a.*
———   do.   Frank.
Chetwynd, Rich'd Walter Chetwynd. *a.*
Churchill, Francis Spencer. First Baron. Frank.
Clinton, Robert Trefusis. Sixteenth Baron.
Clonmore, Lord. *a.*
Colchester, Chas. Abbot. First Baron.
Colville, John Colville. Tenth Baron.
———   do.   Frank.
Boston, Fred. Irby. Second Baron. *a.*
Combermere, Stapleton Cotton. First Baron.
Crewe, John. First Baron.
Dacre, Thos. Brand. Nineteenth Baron.
———   do.   Frank.
De Clifford, Edward Southerd Clifford.
De Dunstanville, Francis Basset. First Baron.

De La Mere, Thomas Cholmondley. First Baron. Frank.
De La Zouche, Cecil Bishopp.
Delvin, Lord. Now Marquess of Westmeath.
De Ross, Charlotte Fitzgerald. Third Baroness. *a.*
Dorchester, Arthur Henry Carleton.
Douglass, Archibald Stewart. First Baron.
Ducie, Thos. Reynolds Norton. Fourth Baron.
Dufferin and Clamboye, James Stevenson Blackwood. First Baron.
Dundas, Laurence.
———— Thomas.
Dynevor, George Talbot Rice.
Ellenborough, Edward Law. First Baron.
———— Edw. Law. Second Baron.
Erskine, Thomas. First Baron. Portrait. *a.*
Fitz Williams, Richard. Seventh Baron. *a.*
Foley, Thomas. Third Baron.
Forbes, James Ochoncar. Seventeenth Baron.
Forester, John George Weld Forester. First Baron.

VOLUME VIII.

Gambier, Jas. First Baron. Admiral.
Gardner, Admiral Lord. *a.*
Glandore, John Crosbie.
Glastonbury, James Grenville. First Baron.
Glenbervie, Sylvester Douglas. First Baron. Portrait.
Glenlyon, James Murray. First Baron.
Grantham, Thomas Philip Robinson. Third Baron. *a.*
———— Lady Grantham, his wife.
Grantley, William Norton. Second Baron. *a.*
———— do.
Gray, Francis. Fifteenth Baron.
Grenville, William Wyndham. First Baron. Portrait.
———— do. Portrait. *a.*
Gwydyr, Peter Robert Burrell. Second Baron.
Haberton, Henry Pomeroy. Second Baron. *a.*
Harris, William George. First Baron. Portrait.
Hawarden, Cornwallis Maude. Third Viscount, and Baroness de Montalt, his wife.
Hawke, Edward William. Third Baron.
Hill, Rowland. First Baron. Portrait.
Holland, Henry R. Vassal Fox. Third Baron. *a.*
———— Lady Holland, his wife.
Howard of Effingham, Kenett Alexander. Eleventh Baron.
Howard De Walden, Chas. Aug. Ellis.
Hutchinson, John Hely. First Baron. Portrait.
Keith, George Keith Elphinstone. First Baron.
———— Miss Elphinstone, his daughter.
Kenyon, George. Second Baron.
Kerry, Francis Thomas Fitzmaurice.
Kilwarden, Lord.
King, Peter. Seventh Baron.
Le Despencer, Thomas Stapleton. Sixteenth Baron. *a.*
Lilford, Thomas Atherton Powys. Second Baron. *a.*
Longford, Thomas Packenham. Third Baron. *a.*
Lovaine, George Percy. *a.*
Lynedoch, Thomas Graham. First Baron. *a.*
Lyttleton, Wm. Henry. Third Baron. *a.*
Manners, Thomas Manners Sutton. First Baron.
Maryborough, W. Wellesley Pole. First Baron. *a.*
Middleton, Henry Willoughby. Sixth Baron.
———— Lady Jane Lauley, his wife. *a.*
Montagu, Henry James. Second Baron.

Montfort, Henry Broomley. Third Baron. a.
Northwick, John Rushout. Second Baron.
—— do. a.
Oriel, John Foster. First Baron.
Palmerston, Henry John Temple. a.
Prudhoe, Algernon Percy. First Baron.
Ranelagh, Thomas Heron Jones. a.
Ravensworth, Thomas Henry Liddell. First Baron.
Redesdale, John Mitford. First Baron.
Ribblesdale, Thomas Lister. First Baron.
Rivers, George Pitt. First Baron. a.
Rodney, George. Third Baron. a.
Rotte, John. Second Baron.
St. Helens, Alleyne Fitz Herbert. First Baron.
Saltown, Alexander George Frazer. Sixteenth Baron.
—— Lady Saltown, his wife. a.
Saye and Sele, Gregory Finnis. Eleventh Baron.
Scarsdale, Nathaniel Curzon. First Baron.
Seaforth, Francis Mackenzie. First Baron.
Selsey, Henry John Peachey. Second Baron.
Sherborne, John Dutton. Second Baron.
Sinclair, Charles St. Clair.
Somerville, John. Fifteenth Baron. Portrait.
Stourton, William. Seventh Baron.
Stowell, William Scott. a. Portrait.
Suffield, Edward Harbord. Third Baron.
Teynham, John Roper. Thirteenth Baron. Frank.
Thurlon, Edward Howell. Second Baron. Frank.
Vernon, Hy. Venables Vernon. Third Baron. Frank.
Walsingham, George De Grey. Third Baron. a.

Willoughby De Broke, Henry Peto Verney. Eighth Baron. Frank.
Yarborough, Charles Anderson Pelham. First Baron.
—— do.

VOLUME IX.

Baronets.

Acland, Sir Thomas Dyke. Tenth Baronet.
Agar, Sir Felix. a.
Aston, Willoughby. a.
Beaumont, George Howland. Seventh Baronet. a.
Bernard, Thomas. a.
—— Lady Bernard, his wife. a.
Boughey, John Fenton Fletcher. Second Baronet. a.
Brooke, Sir Richard. Sixth Baronet. a.
Bunbury, Sir Chas. Sixth Baronet. a.
Bunbury, Sir Henry Edward. Seventh Baronet. a.
Burnett, Robert. Seventh Baronet. a.
Carew, Reginald Pole.
Chetwode, John. Fourth Baronet. a.
Cholmeley, Montagu. First Baronet.
Clarke, Simon. Ninth Baronet. a.
Congreve, William. Second Barnet.
Coote, Eyre. a.
Cornewal, Lady Jane Naper, wife of Sir George. a.
Crichton, Alexander,
Dolben, English. Fourth Baronet.
—— William. Third Baronet. a.
Drake, Francis. a.
Elton, Abraham. a.
Hammond, Andrew Snap. a.
Harding, Henry. Now Lord Hardinge, a distinguished General.
Hartwell, Francis John. First Baronet.
Hastings, Charles. Lt.-General.
Haye, Sir William. Second Baronet.
Gunning, George. Second Baronet.
Hume, Abraham. Second Baronet.
Kennaway, John. First Baronet.
Knatchbull, Edward. Ninth Baronet.

Knighton, Lady Dorothea, wife of Sir William. *a.*
Lennard, Thos. Barret. First Baronet.
Lushington, Lady Hester Boldero, wife of Sir Stephen. *a.*
Mackworth, Digby. Third Baronet. *a.*
Murray, John. Sixth Baronet.
Nugent, George. First Baronet.
Popham, E. H.
––––– Lady Popham, his wife.
Rich, Rev. Sir Charles. Eleventh Baronet. *a.*
Ridley, Mathew.
Shelley, John. Sixth Baronet.
Swinburne, John. Sixth Baronet. *a.*
Sykes, Mark Masterman. Third Baronet. *a.*
Thompson, Charles. First Baronet. *a.*
Thorold, John. Ninth Baronet. *a.*
Wrottesley, John. Ninth Baronet. *a.*

Military and Naval Characters.

Calvert, Sir Harry. *a.*
Dundas, Sir Laurence.
Fawcett, Sir William. *a.*
Ferguson, R. C.
Hope, Sir Alexander. *a.*
Phipps, Edmund.
Picton, Sir Thomas. *a.* Portrait.
Rowley, Major-General. *a.*
Tarleton, General. *a.*
Thornton, Lieut.-General. *a.*
Berry, Sir Edward. Captain. Port. *a.*
Bickerton, Sir Richard. Admiral. *a.*
Bowen, James. Commissioner.
Bridport, Alex. Hood. First Vis. *l. s.*
Coffin, Sir Isaac. Admiral. *a.*
Curzon, Hon. Henry. Vice-Admiral.
Gambier, James. First Lord.
Hood, Sir Samuel. First Baron. Port.
Keats, Sir Richard Goodwin. Portrait.
Kingsmill, Vice-Admiral. *a.*
Nelson and Bronte, Horatio. Facsimile. 2 Portraits.
Pellew, Sir Edward. Viscount Exmouth. Portrait.
Peyton, Rear Admiral. *a.*
Pierrepont, Admiral. *a.*

Popham, Sir Home. Rear Admiral.
Stephens, Sir Philip. Portrait.
St. Vincent, Sir John Jervis. First Earl. Portrait. *a.*
Warre, Henry. Vice-Admiral. *a.*
Young, Sir William. Vice-Admiral. *a.*

VOLUME X.

Public Men.

Abbot, Charles. Speaker (Lord Colchester). *a.* Portrait.
Adams, W. D. Sec. to Rt. Hon. W. Pitt.
Addington, Hiley.
Addington, Mary, wife of the preced'g
Arbuthnot, Geo. Treasury Chambers.
Backhouse, John. Foreign Office.
Baring, Sir Thomas.
Barrow, Sir John. Secretary of the Admiralty.
Bathurst, Charles. Chanceller Duchy of Lancaster. *a.*
Becket, J. Whitehall. *a.*
Bennett, Henry Gray, M.P.
Blackburne, J. J., M.P.
Bloomfield, Gen. Sir Benjamin. Now Lord Bloomfield.
Bond, Rt. Hon. Nathaniel
––––– Phineas, Consul-Genl., Amer.
Boughton, William E. Rouse, M.P.
Bourne, William Sturges. Frank.
Brogden, James, M.P.
Brooksbank, C. C. Sec. to Lord Liverpool. *a.*
Brougham, Henry Lord.
Browne, Dennis, M.P.
Burdett, Sir Francis. Portrait.
––––– Lady Burdett, his wife.
Bute, John. First Marquess. Minister. Portrait. *a.*
Burke, Right Honorable. Portrait.
Butterworth, Jos., M.P.
Byng, George, M.P.
Clacraft, John.
Canning, George. Portrait. *a.*
Canning, Stratford. Ambassador to the Porte. *a.*

Carew, Richard Pole. *a.*
Castlereagh, Lord. Portrait. *a.*
Chester, Sir Robert. *a.*
Coke, Thomas W.
Colebrooke, Henry.
Conant, Sir Nathaniel.
Cooper, Richard Bransby, M.P. *l. s.*
Courtenay, John, M.P. *a.*
Craddock, Henry. Of the Horse Guards, now Lord Howden.
Creweg.
Croker, John Wilson. Sec. to the Admiralty. Portrait.
Davis, Richard Hart, M.P.
Denison, Jos. E., M.P.
——— William.
Dickenson, William, M.P.
Dorrington, John. Clerk of the Fees of the House of Commons. *a.*
Egerton, John Grey, M.P.
Elliott, Right Honorable.
Ellis, Honorable George Agar.
Escourt, Thomas Grimston.
Farquhar.
Fawkes, Walter. *a.*
——— do.
Fitz-Gerald, William Visey.
Flint, Sir Charles W. Allen Office. *a*
——— do.
Fox, Hon. Chas. James. Port.—Frank.
Frazer, T.
Freeling, George Henry. Baronet. General Post Office.
Freemantle, Right Honorable William Henry, M.P.
Frere, John Hookham.
GILBERT, Davis.
GLADSTONE, John.
GOULBORNE, Henry. Minister.
——— Edward.
Grant, Robert M. P. Elgin.
——— R. Dublin. *a.*
——— Charles. Board of Trade.
——— John Peter, M.P.
Grenfell, Pascoe, M.P. Marlow.
Grenville, Thomas.
Hamilton, Terrick. Diplomatist.
Hammond, Sir Andrew Snape.

Hardinge, Sir Henry. Now Lord Hardinge.
Harrison, George. Treasury. *a.*
——— do. *a.*
——— do. *a.*
Hatsell, John. Clerk of the House of Commons.
Harvey, Captain. Secretary to the late Duke of Kent. *a.*
Heber, Richard. Book Collector.
Hobhouse, Henry, M.P.
——— Sir Benjamin.
Hoblyn, Thomas.
HORNER, Francis, M.P.
HUME, Joseph, M.P. Portrait.
HUSKISSON, William, M.P. *a.*
JEKYLL, Joseph.
KNATCHBULL, Sir Edward.

VOLUME XI.

Lamb, George, M.P.
Lambton, John G. (Earl of Durham.)
Latouche, John, M.P.
Legge, Henry. Navy Office. *a.*
Leicester, Sir John Fleming. Portrait.
Locker, John. Greenwich Hospital.
Long, Right Honorable Charles. Army Pay Office. *a.*
Lowe, Sir Hudson. *a.*
Lushington, Sir Stephen R. *a.*
McGregor, Sir James. Army Medical Board. *a.*
MACKINTOSH, Sir James. *a.* Portrait.
——— Lady Mackintosh, his wife. *a.*
MACMAHON, Sir John.
Manning, William.
MARRIOTT, George W.
MERRY, Anthony. American Minister.
MOORE, Graham.
Manning, William, M.P.
Newport, Sir John.
NOEL, Honorable Francis J.
Paget, Honorable Berkeley, M.P. *a.*
PEEL, Sir Robert.
PERCIVAL, Spencer. Portrait.
Petit, Louis Hayes.
Petrie, Henry.

Phillips, E. Sec. to the Speaker. *a.*
PITT, Rt. Hon. William. Portrait. *a.*
Plumer, Sir William.
POLE, Wellesley. *a.*
Ponsonby, W. S.
Powell, Sheriff for Kent. *a.*
Powell, Sir John Kynaston.
Putteney, Sir William. *a.*
Ricardo, David, M.P. *a.*
Rice, Thomas Spring, M.P.
Riddle, Edw. Naval Asylum, Greenw.
Robinson, Fred. John. Lord Goderich.
―― George.
Rose, Right Hon. George. *a.* Portrait.
―― his wife. *a.*
―― William Stewart.
―― Miss Rose, his sister. *a.*
Rumbold, Charles E., M.P.
Sargent, William.
SHERIDAN, Richard Brinsley. Portrait.
Sinclair, Sir John. Portrait. *a.*
―― George. *a.*
Smith, William, M.P.
―― Hon. Robert, M.P.
―― William. Ambassador.
Smyth, J.P., M.P.
Stewart, Sir Charles. Ambassador. *a.*
Sullivan, John.
Sutton, Charles Manners. *a.*
Sykes, Sir Mark Mastermann.
Taylor, George Watson.
Tierney, George.
Tyrwhitt, Sir Thomas.
Vansittart, Right Hon. Nicholas. Lord Bexley. *a.* Portrait.
―― Lady Sarah, his wife.
Vaughan, Sir Robert W., M.P.
Vernon, Granville Venables, M.P.
Wall, Charles Baring.
Wallace, Right Honorable Thomas. Portrait. *a.*
Ward, Robert. Of the Admiralty.
Wardle, G. L. Portrait.
Warrender, Sir George.
Watts, David Pike.
Wharton, Robert. Author.
WHITBREAD, Samuel, M.P. Portrait.
Whitbread, Samuel, Jr. *a.*
―― do.

Wickman, Right Hon. William. *a.*
WILBERFORCE, William, M.P. Portrait.
―― do.
―― R. A.
WILBRAHAM, Roger. Book Collector.
―― Edward Booth.
―― do.
―― his wife. *a.*
WILKES, John. Portrait.
Willmott, R. Sec. to Lord Liverpool.
―― Downing Street. *a.*
Wilson, Sir Robert, M.P. *a.*
―― W. W. Carus, M.P.
―― Gloucester.
Wyndham, Right Honorable. *a.*
Yorke, Sir Jarip. *a.*
―― do. *a.*

VOLUME XII.

Men of the Robe.

Arden, Sir Richard Pepper. Lord Alvanley. *a.*
Bailey, Sir John. *a.*
Borrough, Sir James.
Chambre, Sir Allen. *d. s.*
Dallas, Sir Robert.
ELDON, John Scott. Portrait.
ELLENBOROUGH, Edward Law. First Baron. Portrait.
Eyre, Chief Baron.
Garrow, Sir William. Portrait. *a.*
Gibbs, Sir Vicary. Portrait. *a.*
Gould, Sir Henry. *d. s.*
Grant, Sir William.
Kenyon, Lord. *a.*
Leach, Sir John. *a.*
MANSFIELD, William. First Earl. Port.
Moore. Judge of the Common Pleas, Ireland.
Nares, G.
Park, Sir James. *a.*
―― Sir James Allan. *a.*
Plumer, Sir Thomas. *a.*
Richards, Sir R. *a.*
Scott, Sir William. Portrait.

Adam, William. Counsel. *a.*
Bell, J. Chancery Barrister. *a.*
Brougham, Henry. Portrait. *a.*
Butler, Charles.
Christian.
Clarke, Longueville. Barrister.
Comyn, Samuel.
Denman, Thomas. *a.* Portrait.
Gifford, Sir Robert. *a.*
Heald. *a.*
Heywood, Sergeant. *a.*
Hill, Sergeant. *a.*
Jekyll, Joseph. *a.*
Leycester, Hugh.
Manley, Sergeant. *a.*
Phillimore, Dr.
Phillips, Charles. Portrait.
Pollock, Fred.
Praed, William Mackworth.
Robert, William.
——— do.
Rotch, Barrister. *a.*
ROMILLY, Sir Samuel. Portrait. *a.*
SCARLETT, Sir James. *a.*
Skirron, Walter. Counsellor.
Stephen, James.
SUGDEN, Sir Edward.
WISHAU, J.
Wigley. Of the Temple.
Wilson, R.

Cannon, Edward. St. Georges, Hanover Square.
Chapman. *a.*
Crosby, Robt. Rector of Shoreditch.
Cunningham, F.
——— J. W. Harrow.
Dallin, R. Greenwich.
Dealtry, William Clapham.
Dennis, Prebend.
D'Oyley, George, D.D. Lambeth.
Ellis, J. E.
Fallowfield, Dr. J. St. Pancras.
Fisher, Philip, D.D. Chart. House. *a.*
Foster. Clerkenwell. *a.*
Gilbert, A. T.
Goddard. Brampton Lecturer.
Goodall, J., D.D. Provost of Eton.
Gurney, William B. Essex, St.
HEBER, Reginald. Bishop of Calcutta.
Hill, Thomas.
——— J. Master of Merchant Tailor's. *a.*
Lloyd, C., D.D.
Mann, Wm. St. Saviour's, Southw'k.
Mathias, William. Whitechapel.
Nunn, William. St. Clements, Manchester.
Owen, John Fulham.
——— do.
——— do.
——— C.
Pratt, Josiah. Coleman Street.
Randolph, J., D.D. Bristol.
Reed, Andrew. Cannon Street.
RUDGE, James. Limehouse. Port.
Russell, J. D. D. Bishopgate.
RICHMOND, Legh.
Schwabb, E.
Shepherd, G. Bloomsbury.
Sheppard, Thomas. Pentonville.
Simeon, Charles. Cambridge. *a.*
Stewart, James H.
Valentine, William. Lond. Hosp.
Venn, Henry. St. Dunstan's.
Valpy, Richard, D.D. Reading. *a.*
Warren, Dawson. Edmonton.
Watkins, Henry. London Stone. *a.*
——— do.

VOLUME XIII.

Clergy of the Establishment.

Ackland, Rev. J. C.
Andrewes.
Atwood, T. S.
Barrow, William.
Bean, James. British Museum. *a.*
BICKERSTETH, E. Church Miss'y.
Black, W. H.
Bowerbank, Thomas. Chiswick.
Buchanan, Claudius, D.D. Port. *a.*
Budd, Henry. Bridewell Hospital.
Burney, Charles, D.D.
Butler, S., D.D. Shrewsbury.
Calvert, T. Morrissean, Prof. Camb.

Whildale. Westminster, Spital-Fields. *a.*
Wilcox, S. Little Shoreham, Suffolk.
Wilson, Daniel. Islington.
Yates, Richard. Chelsea Hospital.

VOLUME XIV.

Church of Scotland and Non-Conforming Divines.

CHALMERS, Thomas, D.D. Port. *a.*
Fletcher, Alexander. Finsbury.
Irving, Edward. Portrait.
Waugh, Alexander, D.D. Portrait.

Adkins, Thos. Southampton. Port.
Berry, J. Hackney.
Bull, Thomas P. Newport Pagnett. Portrait.
BURDER, George. Fetter Lane.
―――― do.
―――― Henry Foster. Hackney. Portrait.
Campbell, John Kingsland. Portrait.
CLARKE, Adam. Portrait.
Clayton, John. do.
―――― George. do.
Collison, George.
COLLYER, William. Bengo. Port.
―――― do.
Cox, F. A. Hackney.
Dewhirst, Charles. Bury.
Dyer, John. Reading.
Evanson, Edward. Reading.
Ford, George. Mile End.
Frey, C. F.
Greig, George.
Griffin, John. Portsea.
HILL, Rowland. Portrait.
Harris, William. Hoxton.
Hughes, Joseph. Battersea.
Humphrys, John.
Hyatt, John. Pentonsville.
INNES, William. Edinburgh.
―――― John.

Ivimey, Joseph.
Knight. Ponders-End.
Leifchild, John. Kensington.
Lewis, Thomas. Islington.
Lowell, Samuel. Bristol.
McAll, R. S.
Mann, John Bermondsey.
Newman, William. Bow.
Palmer, Samuel. Hackney.
Priestley, William.
Pugsley, N. H. Stockport.
RAFFLES, Thos. Liverpool. Port.
RIPPON, John. Baptist.
Roby, William. Manchester.
Rowe, W. H. Weymouth.
Ryland, John. Bristol.
Smith, John Pye.
Thomas, John. Highgate.
Thorpe, William. Richmond.
Townley, Charles. Newington. *a.*
―――― Henry.
―――― do.
Townsend, John Bermondsey.
Vint, William. Of Idle.
Wardlaw, George. Blackburn.
Warren, Samuel. Wesleyan.
Watson, Richard. do.
Wilks, Matthew. Portrait.
Winter, Robert.
Worthington, Hugh.

Aspland, Robert. Hackney.
Belsham, Thomas. Essex Street. *a.*
Butcher, Edmund.
Carpenter, Dr. L.
Dsiney, John. A distinguished Divine and Magistrate.
Evans, John. Islington. Miscellaneous Writer.
Fox, William J. Finsbury.
Lindsay, J. Bow.
Lindsay, Theophilus. Essex Street. Eminent Unitarian Minister and Writer.
REES, Abraham. Portrait.
Rees, Thomas.

VOLUME XV.

Poets and Dramatic Writers.

ADDISON, Joseph. Portrait.
Ansley, Christopher.
——— Arthur. Pleader's Guide.
Arnold, Samuel. Dramatist.
BLOOMFIELD, Robert. Two Portraits.
BOWRING, John.
CAMPBELL, Thomas. Portrait.
Cary, H. F. Translator of Dante.
Coleman, George, Jr. Portrait.
COLERIDGE, S. T. do.
CRABBE, George. do.
Croly, George.
CUNNINGHAM, Allan.
DIBDIN, Charles. Portrait.
——— do. Jr.
——— Thomas. Two portraits.
Dimond, William. Dramatist.
DuBois, Edward.
Elton, Charles A. Translator of Hesiod Poet.
FALCONER, William. The Shipwreck.
Gent, Thomas.
GIFFORD, William. Portraits.
Good, John Mason. Trans. Lucretius.
HOOK, Theodore Portrait.
HOOLE, John. Translator of Tasso and Ariosto.
LAMB, Charles.
Leigh, Chandos.
MALONE, Edmund. Portrait.
MONCRIEFF, W. T. Dramatist.
Mooney, William. *a.*
MOORE, Thomas. Portrait. *a.*
MURPHY, Arthur. do. *a.*
POPE, Alexander. Two portraits.
Pratt, Samuel J. Portrait.
PROCTOR, R. W., *alias* Barry Cornwall.
Pye, Henry James. Portrait.
REED, Isaac. do.
Reynolds, Frederick. do.
Ritson, Joseph. Ancient Poetry.
ROGERS, Samuel. Portrait.
Rose, William Stewart.
Mathias, Thomas. *a.*
Sargent, John.
SCOTT, Sir Walter. Portrait.

SHELLY, Percy Bysshe.
SMITH, Horace. } Rejected Addresses.
——— James. }
Soane, George. Dramatist.
Sotheby, William. Oberon.
SOUTHEY, Robert. Portrait.
Spencer, W. R.
Stevens, George.
SWIFT. Autograph wanting. Port.
Thurlow, Edward. Second Baron.
Townsend, George. Armageddon.
WARTON, Thomas. Portrait.
Wemyss, Richard.
Wiffin, J. H.
WORDSWORTH, William. Portrait.

VOLUME. XVI.

Dramatic Performers.

Abbott, William. Of Covent Garden Theatre.
BANNISTER, John. Portrait.
Bishop, Henry R. *a.*
BRAHAM, John.
BROADHURST, William.
BUNN, Mrs. Portrait.
Carew, Miss do.
Cooper, John. do.
Copeland, Frances Eliz. Portrait.
Cubitt, Maria.
Dickson, Sarah. *a.*
Dowton, William.
Duruset, John.
Edwin, Elizabeth Rebecca. Portrait.
ELLISTON, R. W. Portrait.
Farley, Charles. do.
Farren, William. do.
GARRICK, David. Portrait.
Glover, Julia.
Grimaldi, Joseph.
Grove, D.
HARLEY, J. P. Two Portraits.
HORN, Charles E. Portrait.
HULL, Thomas. do
Johnson, Henry E.
JOHNSON, Dorothy. Portrait.
KEAN, Edward. do

KELLY, Michael. Portrait.
—— Frances M. do
—— Lydia.
KEMBLE, John Philip. Two Portraits.
—— Stephen. Portrait.
—— Charles. Two Portraits.
King, Thomas. do do
Knight, Edward. Portrait.
Lacy, Drury Lane Theatre.
Egerton, Daniel.

VOLUME XVII.

Macauley, Elizabeth W.
MOUNTAIN, Rose. Portrait.
MUNDEN, Joseph S. Two Portraits.
O'NEILL, Miss E. Portrait.
Orger, M. A. do
OXBERRY, William. do
PAYNE, John Howard.
Peake, Richard.
Phillips, R.
Pope, Alexander.
Powell, John.
Quick, J. Two Portraits.
Robertson, Henry,
Russell, S. T. Portrait.
SIDDONS, Sarah. Portrait.
Smith, George. Two Portraits.
Smithen, Miss.
STEPHENS, Catherine. Portrait.
Taylor, Charles. Two Portraits.
Terry, Daniel. Portrait.
Tree, Anne M. do
—— M. do
VESTRIS, Eliza. do
Welsh, Thomas.
Winston, John. do
WROUGHTON, Richard.
Yates, Fred. H.
Young, Charles Mayne. Portrait.

Musical Composers.

Addison, John.
Attwood, Thomas.
Cooke, Thomas.
Corri, D.
CROTCH, William. Mus. D. Portrait.
Hague, O.

Nicholson, Chas.
Parry, John.
Reeve, William. Portrait.
Shield, William.
SMART, Sir Geo.
Smart, H.
WESLEY, Samuel. Eminent Composer. Nephew of Dr. Wesley.
Whitfield, J. C.

VOLUME XVIII.

Authors.

Abbot, Charles. "Flora Bedfordienses."
AIKIN, John. M.D. *a*. Portrait.
—— Arthur. Chemical Dictionaey.
AINSWORTH, H. H, Manchester.
Ainton, W. Eminent Botanist. *a*.
Andrews, James Pettit. Miscellaneous Writer. *a*. Portrait.
Bacon, Wm. M.
Baily, Francis. *a*.
Baker, George. History of Northamptonshire.
Bancroft, Dr. Edward. *N. a.*
Banim, John. Novelist.
BARROW, John. Baronet.
—— Doctor Wm.
Bellamy, John. Hebraist.
Beloe, William. "Sexgenarian," etc.
Bennett, Wm. "Constancy of Israel," etc.
BENTHAM, Jeremy. *a*.
BIGLAND, John. *a*.
Bingley, William. Naturalist.
Blakeaway, J. B. "History of Shrewsbury."
Blarequie, Edward.
Bliss, Doctor Philip.
Bott, E.
Bowdler, Thomas.
BOWRING, John.
Bramsen, John. Travels, etc.
Bray, William. History of Surrey.
Brayley, Edward Wedloke. "Beauties of England and Wales, etc.

Brewer, James Norris. Miscellaneous Writer.
Bridge, D. Mathematician.
Britton, John. Portrait.
Brown, Robert. Botanist.
BROWNE, Isaac Hawkins. "Essays."
―――― do
―――― S. Traveller.
Bryant, Jacob. Portrait. "An author of uncommon learning and research."
BUCKLAND, William.
Bulleck, William. "Travels in Mexico."
Burney, Dr. Charles. Portrait.
―――― do
―――― do
―――― Dr. Charles Parr. n.
―――― do
Barrow, Dr. E. J. Divine and Miscellaneous Writer.
Butler, Charles. Miscellaneous Writer.
―――― Dr., of Harrow.
―――― Rev. Dr. of Shrewsbury, Editor of Æschylus, etc.
Caley, John. Antiquary.
Campbell, Laurence Dundas.
Cambridge, Archdeacon.
Carr, Sir John. Portrait.
Chalmers, Alexander.
Christie, James. Antiquary.
Churchyard, Thomas.
Churton, Rev. R.
Clarke, James Stanier.
―――― do
CLARKE, Edward Daniel.
―――― William. Gray's Inn.
Cogan, Thomas. Theological and Philosophical Writer.
Colebrooke, H. Miscellaneous Writer.
Coleridge, H.
Collier, John Payne. "History of the Stage." "Life of Shakespeare," etc.
Combe, George. Phrenologist.
Conder, Joseph. Miscellaneous Writer.
Connolly, Dr. Strafford on Avon.
Copley, D. E.
Coxe, Rev. William. Historian. Portrait.

―――― Miss E. H., his sister.
Crawford, Robert.
Crawford, Quinten. "History of the Hindoos" and other Works.
Croly, Rev. George.
Crombie, Alexander. Writer on Philology and Theology.
Cromwell, Thomas. "Life of Cromwell" and other Works.
Crowe, E. S.
Cunningham, Allan.
―――― J. W. Theologian.

VOLUME XIX.

Dallas, R. C. Miscellaneous Writer.
Darley, George.
Davies, Edward. Antiquarian.
Dealtry, Dr. W. "On Fluxion," etc.
DELOLME, John. Portrait.
De Reazy, S .Sparrow.
DIBDIN, Tho. Frognall. Portrait.
D'ISRAELI, J. Portrait.
Douce, Francis.
Douglas, William. a.
DRAKE, Nathan. Portrait. a.
Drury, Henry. Essayist. a.
Du Bois, Edward. "The Wreath" and other Works.
Dunster, Rev. Chas. "Notes on Milton," etc
Dyer, George. History of Cambridge." Portrait.
Edgworth, Richard Lovell.
Ellis, Henry. a.
EMERSON, Wm. A very Eminent Mathematician.
Engelback, L. G.
Englefield. Sir Henry. Portrait.
Ensor, George. Economist. Independent Men."
Eton, William. "Survey of Turkey."
Faulkner, Thomas. "History of Chelsea" and of other Places.
Fisher, Thomas. "Antiquities of Warwickshire," etc.
Foster, Thomas. "Perennial Calendar and other Works.

FOSBROOKE, Thomas D. Antiquarian.
FOSCOLO, Ugo.
Fox, William.
FRANCKLIN, William. "Historical Works on India."
—— Col. Tour to Shiraz.
Frend, William. "Evening Amusements."
Gage, Jno. "Antiquities of Suffolk," etc.
GALT, John. Portrait.
Gifford, John. "History of France."
Gilchrist. Octavius. Bibliography and Criticism.
GILLIES, Dr. John. History of Greece. Portrait.
Gisborne, Rev. Thomas. Theologian.
Goldsmith, Lewis. Historian and Libeller.
GODWIN, William. *a.* Portrait.
GOOD, John Mason.
Graham, Rev. G. G. Local History.
——— do
Graves, George. Naturalist.
Hall, Sidney.
——— Basil.
HALLAM, Henry.
Hamper, William. "Life of Dugdale."
HARRIS, James. Eminent Philologist. Father of Lord Malmsbury." Portrait.
Hay, John Allan. Life of Wallace.
Haigarth. Bush Life in Australia.
Hervé, Peter. "How to Enjoy Paris."
GRATTAN, T. C. Historian and Naturalist.
Hewetson, W. B.
HOARE, Prince. Two Portraits.
——— Sir Richard Colt.
HONE, William. Portrait.
Hooke, S. Account of Bristol.
HORNE, Thomas Hartwell.
HOWARD, John. Two Portraits.
HUNT, Leigh.
Hunt, Henry Leigh, son of the preceding.
——— John, brother of Leigh.
Hunter, John. History of Hallamshire.
Huntingford, Henry. Editor of Pindar.

Hutton, George.
HUTTON, Dr. Charles. Two Portraits.
——— do
——— do
——— do
——— Charles, his son. General. Announcing his Father's Death.

VOLUME XX.

Illingworth, Cayley.
IRELAND, William Henry. Portrait.
IRVING, Washington. do
JEFFREY, Francis, do
Jerdan, William. "Literary Gazette."
Joddrell, R. P. Philologist and Poet.
JOHNSON, Dr. Samuel. Portrait. *a.*
JONES, Sir William. do *a.*
——— Lady A. M. Jones, his wife. *a.*
——— do *a.*
Kelly, Patrick. Cambist.
Kett, Patrick. "Emily" and other Works.
Kidd, Thomas. "Porsonia."
Kitchiner, Dr. William.
Konig, Charles. "Annals of Botany."
LAMB, Charles
Lambert, A. Bourk. Botanical. *a.*
——— "Life of Bishop Waynefleet."
Latham, John. Ornithologist.
LAUDERDALE, Earl of. On PublicWealth and on Indian Government.
Leach, Dr. *a.*
Lemaitre, J. G. Author of "Letters of Sir Charles Darnley," etc.
Lempriere, Dr. I. "Classical Dictionary."
LINGARD, John. Historian. *a.*
LODGE, Edmund.
Longmate, Barrack. Herald.
LOUDON, J. C. Botanist.
Lowe, J. Political Economy.
Luders, Henry. Jurist and Historian.
McHenry, L. Grammarian.
MACKINTOSH, Sir James. Portrait. *a.*
Magee, Dr. Dean of Cork. Theologian.

Malham, John. Miscellaneous Writer.
Markland, John Hy.
Marsden, William. " History of Sumatra."
—— do
Marshall, John. " Naval Biography."
MASERES, Francis. Mathematician and Miscellaneous Writer.
Matthew Henry. *a.*
MAURICE, Thomas. Histories and Indian Antiquities. *a.*
MAWE, John. Mineralogist. " Travels in Brazil."
Mayne, John. Star Office.
Merle, Gibbons. Sketches of France.
MEYRICK, Samuel R. "Ancient Armour."
Millard, John. Surrey Institution.
Millingen, John.
MILLS, Charles. "History of the Crusades," etc.
MITCHELL, T. Translator of Aristophanes.
MITFORD, W. Historian.
—— John. Editor of Gray's Poems, etc. *a.*
Monk, J. H. Greek Professor. Camb.
Montagu, Basil. *u.*
Morgan, B. S. *a.*
—— Thomas.
—— William.
—— Sir T. Charles.
MORRISON, Robert. To J. Reeves and latter's answer.
Mulford, William. Editor of the Courier.
—— do
Muloch, Thomas. "Highlands and Islands of Scotland considered." *a.*
MURRAY, Lindley. Portrait.
Myers, T. Geographer.

VOLUME XXI.

Nares, Robert. "Elements of Orthoepy," etc.
NICHOLS, John. Miscellaneous and most voluminous Writer and Editor. Two Portraits.
Nichols, John Bowyer. Son of the preceding.
NICOLAS, Sir Nicholas Harris.
Noehden, G. N.
O'Conor, Charles. Of Stowe.
O'Hanlon, H. M.
O'MEARA, Barry.
Orme, Robert. Historian, Portrait.
Ormerod, George. do *a.*
OUSELEY, Sir William. Portrait.
Palemon.
Park, Thomas.
Parker, Thomas Lester. Antiquary.
Parkinson, Jas. "Organic Remains." *a.*
PARR, Dr. Samuel. Portrait.
Patmore, George. Periodical Writer. Second to John Scott in his fatal Duel.
PENNANT, Thomas. Portrait.
Perry, James. Editor of the Morning Chronicle. Portrait.
Petrie. *a.*
PHILLIPS, Sir Richard.
—— William. Mineralogist. *a.*
Piggott, Rev. Solomon.
PINKERTON, John. Portrait.
Picquet, A. Elementary Works.
Plantà, Jos. Helvetia Confederacy. *a.*
PLAYFAIR, William.
Plumtre, Rev. John.
POLWHETE, Richard.
POTTER, Richard. Translator of Euripides.
PRATT, S. J. Miscellaneous Writer. Portrait.
Preston Wm. Illustrations of Masonry. Portrait.
PROCTOR, Barry. (Barry Cornwall.)
Pugen, Augustus.
Rede, W. L.
REES, Dr. Abraham. Portrait.
Reeves, John. Historian. *a.* Portrait.
Reed, Dr.
Reynolds, T. Britanniarum.
Reynolds, J. H.
Ritchie, Andrew.
Robertson, R.
Roots, George. *a.*
Roscoe, William. Portrait.

Roscoe, Henry.
Rose, William Stuart.
Ruding, Rogers.
Ross, Mr. Geographer. a.
Rundle, Thomas. Long Letter by him in the hand writing of Isaac Reed. Portrait of the latter.
Rutt, John Powell.

VOLUME XXII.

SABINE, Joseph. Naturalist.
Saunders, Rev. T. Biographer.
Saunders, William. Medical and other Works. Portrait.
Savage, Wm. Works on Typography.
Scott, John. "Visit to Paris." a.
SEWARD, William. Biography, etc. a. Portrait.
Shepherd, Rev. Wm. Life of Pogger and other Works. Portrait.
Shobert, Fred. Translator from the German and Miscellaneous Writer.
Sidney, J. Francis. "Missionary Priest."
SIMS, John. Eminent Physician and Botanist.
Simpson, Thos. Mathematics. Travels.
—— William. "Journal during the Niger Expedition," etc.
SIMSON, Robert. Eminent Mathematician.
SINCLAIR, Sir John. Portrait.
—— do a.
Smedley, Edw. Editor of "Encyclopedia Metropolitana."
SMITH, James.
—— Horace. a.
Smyth, William. Prof. Camb. Greek and Roman Antiquities, etc.
Somerville, Dr. Thomas. "Reign of Queen Anne." a.
Sowerby, James. Botanist.
Spence, William. Entomologist.
Staunton, Sir George T. a.
Stedman, Rev. Thomas. Shrewsbury.
—— George.

Stevens, M. "Horae Ecclesiasticus." a.
Stewart, Sir James.
Stoddart, Dr. J.
Street. Courier Office.
Stuart, Andrew. "General History of the Stuarts."
Sumner, Bishop Charles R. Theologian.
Surr, Thomas S. Novelist.
Surtees, Robert. Hist. of Co. of Durham.
Symmons, J. "Agamemnon."
TALFOUR, T. N. a.
Taplin, Dr. William. Portrait.
Taylor, William. "English Synonymes" and other Works.
Thelwal, John. Lectures and Polemical Writer.
Thomson, Dr. William. New Annual Register.
—— do
Thornton, Robert John. Botanist. Portrait.
Thomkins, Thomas. Portrait.
Tooke, William. Historian. a.
Toulmin, Joseph. Historian and Theologian.
Townsend, Joseph. "History of Moses."
—— F. Herald.
TREDGOLD, J. Engineer.
TURNER, Sharon. Historian.
—— Dawson. "Tour in Normandy."
Tweddell, Francis.
Twiss, Richard. Travels and Miscellanies.
—— Horace. Portrait.
Utterson, Edward.
VALPY, Dr. Richard.
Van Dyk, H. S.
VINCENT, Dr. Wm. Dean of Westminster. Portrait.
Wade, J. Birmingham.
WALPOLE, Horace. Earl of Oxford. Portrait. a.
Watkins, Henry G. Theologian.
Webb, Cornelius, Essayist.
Windeborn, Dr. Editor of Wm. Penn's Life. a.

WHITE, J. Blanco. Miscellaneous Writer.
WILD, Charles. Architect. *a.*
Wilkins, Dr. Charles. Orientalist.
——— George. "Body and Soul."
Willement, Thomas. Works on Heraldry.
Williams, John B. "Life of M. Henry."
——— Rev. Theodore.
Wood, Manley.
——— William. Naturalist.
Wordsworth, Dr. Christ. Theological Works, Travels, etc.
Wrangham, Rev Francis.
Young, Charles G.

VOLUME XXIII.
Travellers.

BANKS, Sir Joseph. Portrait.
BARROW, John. *a.*
Batty, Capt. Robert,
BELZONI, G. Portrait.
Bowditch, I. E. Travels in Africa.
Browne, William George. do
Buckingham, James S. Mesopotamia,
——— do.
CLARKE, Edward Daniel.
Cockerell, C. R. Greece.
Collins, Captain David. New South Wales. Portrait.
FitzClarence, George. Earl of Munster. Journal of a Route across India.
FRANKLIN, Captain. Portrait.
GELL, Sir William.
HALL, Basil.
HOBHOUSE, John Cam.
Holland, Dr. Travels in Albania, etc.
Hughes, Thomas Smart. Greece.
Jackson, John Gray. Tour to Shiraz. Portrait. *a.*
Jacob, John. Travels in Spain.
Jorgenson, J. France and Germany.
LYON, George. North Pole.
MALCOLM, Sir John.
Mawe, John. Brazil.
OUSELEY, Sir Gore.

PARRY, Captain.
RAFFLES, Sir Stamford.
RICHARDSON, Dr. John.
Ross, Captain John.
SCORESBY, Willam, Jr. Portrait.
Somerville, Dr.
Walpole, Robert. Travels in the East, etc.
Waring, John Scott. "Tour to Shiraz."

VOLUME XXIV.
Medical and Surgical.

Armstrong, Dr., Jno. Pathology.
ARNOT, Neil, M.D. "Elements of Physics," etc.
Babington, William, M.D. Mineralogist.
Bain, Andrew, M.D.
BAILLIE, Matthew, Portrait.
——— do.
Birbeck, George. *a.*
BLANE, Sir Gilbert. On Medical Science, etc. Portrait.
Bostock, John. On Physiology, etc.
BUCHAN, William. 2 portraits.
Burrows, G. M. On Insanity.
Chandler, George.
Conquest, J. T. On Midwifery, etc.
Crichton, Alexander. Works on Physiology, Pathology, etc.
Currie, Dr. James.
Darling, George. Russell Square.
Fitton, W. H. Geologist.
FORDYCE, William.
GOOD, John Mason.
HAWES, William. Founder of the Humane Society and author of Several Works. Portrait.
Haygarth, J.
Hervy, Dr. *a.*
Holland, Dr. N. Travels in Hungary. *a.*
Holme, Edward, of Manchester.
HUNTER, William. Portrait. *a.*
JENNER, Edward. do.
Kerr, J. Of Northampton. *a.*

Kitchener, Dr. J. *a.*
KNIGHTON, Sir William.
Laird, James.
LETTSOM, John Cookley. Portrait. *a.*
Lister, William.
McGREGOR, Sir James. *a.*
Maton, William George. Naturalist.
Marcet, Alexander. Works on Pathology and Chemistry.
Paris, John Ayrton. " Pharmacology."
PEARSON, Dr. George. Author of numerous Works.
Pett, Dr. G. Hackney.
Powell, Robert.
Ramadge, F. H. Therapeutics.
Reeder, Dr. Henry. do. *a.*
Roget, Peter M. Physiology.
Roots, Dr. Of Kingston.
Scott, John. Bedford Square.
Shearman, William. On Chronic Debility, etc.
SIMS, James. Pathology. 2 portraits.
SOLOMON, James. A famous Jewish Quack. "Balm of Gilead," etc. Portrait.
Southey, Henry H. On Pulmonary Consumption.
THOMSON, Thomas. Biographies and numerous Scientific Works. Portrait.
Tuthill, Geo. Leman.
Walker, John. Vaccination.
Yeats, E.
Yelloly, John. On Nervous Diseases.

Surgeons.

ABERNETHY, John. *a.*
ADAMS, Sir William. Oculist.
BELL, Charles. *a.*
BLAIR, William. Great Russell Sq. Numerous Works.
——— do.
——— do.
BLIZARD, Sir William.
BRODIE, B. C.
Carlisle, A. On Old Age. *a.*
Cline, Henry.
COOPER, Sir Astley.
——— do.
——— do.

EARLE, Sir James.
Forster, Thompson. On Aneurism, etc.
Headington, Richard Clement.
HOME, Sir Everard. Anatomy.
Laurence, William. Physiology.
Stanley. Edward.

VOLUME XXV.
Painting.

Allann, Thomas.
Arnold, George. Associate. *a.*
BEECHEY, Sir William, R.A. Portrait.
——— do.
——— Lady. His Wife. *a.*
Buckler, John.
——— John C. His son.
Bigg, William R., R.A.
Bone, Henry, R.A.
CALCOTT, Augustus Wall, R.A.
CHALON, Alfred Edward, R.A.
Clint, George. Associate.
Collins, William. R.A.
Coney, John.
Constable, John, R.A.
Cooper, Abraham, R.A.
Corbauld, Henry.
Craig, William.
CRUIKSHANK, George.
DANIELL, Thomas, R.A. *a.*
DANIELL, William, R.A. *a.*
——— Samuel. *a.*
DAWE, George, R.A.
Devis, A.
DeWent, P. *a.*
——— do.
Derby, William.
DRUMMOND, Samuel. Associate.
Edridge, Henry.
——— do.
EDWARDS, Edward. Portrait.
FARINGTON, Joseph, R.A.
FUSELI, Henry, R.A. Portrait.
Garrard, George. Associate. *a.*
HAMILTON, William, R.A. *a.*
HAYDON, R. R. Portrait.
HAYTER, George.

Hilton, William.
—— do.
HOPPNER, John, R.A.
Howard, Henry, R.A. *a.*
HUMPHREY, Ozias, R.A. Profile. *a.*
JACKSON, John, R.A. Portrait.
Jones, George, R.A.
LAWRENCE, Sir Thomas. Portrait.
—— do. *a.*
—— do. *a.*
Lewis, F. C. Who accompanied T. F. Dibdin in his Continental Tour.
Mee, Mrs. Miniature Painter. *a.*
MULREADY, William.
Nattes, Claude.
NORTHCOTE, James. Portrait.
—— do.
OWEN, William, R.A. Portrait. *a.*
PHILLIPS, Thomas, R.A. Portrait.
—— do.
Pope, Alexander.
Raimbach, A.
Reinagle, Richard Ramsay. Associate.
Renton, John.
REYNOLDS, Sir Joshua. Portrait. *a.*
Rigaud, S.
Sass, Henry.
Satchwell, R. W.
—— do.
SHEE, Martin, P.R.A. Portrait.
SMIRKE, Robert, R.A.
STOTHARD, Thomas, R.A.
—— R. T. His Son.
Thomson, Henry, R.A.
TURNER, Joseph Mallard Wm., R.A.
Unwins, Thomas, Associate. *a.*
—— do.
—— do. *a.*
WARD, James, R.A. *a.*
—— do.
WEST, Benjamin, P.R.A. Portrait.
WESTWALL, Richard, R.A.
Wild, Charles.
—— do.
WILKIE, David, R.A.
—— do.

VOLUME XXVI.
Sculptors.
Bacon, John. Portrait.
Bailey, Edward H.
Behms, William. . *a.*
CHANTREY, Francis. Portrait.
FLAXMAN, John. do. *a.*
Gahagar, S.
Henning, John.
—— do. *a.*
Rossi, Charles.
TURNERELLI, P. Portrait.
WESTMACOTT, Richard. Portrait.

Architects.
Beazley, James.
Brooks, William,
Burton, Decimus.
Cottingham, L. N.
Elmes, James.
Gandy, Joseph.
Gwilt, Joseph.
—— do. *a.*
Holland, Henry.
Laing, David.
Lugars. *a.*
Morrison, R. Of Dublin.
Nash. *a.*
—— Frederick.
Nicholson, Peter.
Porden, William.
Pugin, Augustus.
Smirke, Robert. *a.*
Soane, John. Portrait. *a.*
Stuart, James, (Athenian). Portrait.
Wilkins, William.
Woods, Joseph.
Wyatt, Matthew. Sculptor.
—— James. Portrait.

VOLUME XXVII.
Scientific.
Aikin, Arthur. Dictionary of Chymistry and Mineralogy, etc.
Allen, Willian. Chymist.
Atkinson, Henry William. Royal Mint.

BANKS, Sir Joseph, P.R.S. Portrait.
Bartow, P. On Magnetic Attractions and other works.
Barnouin, James H. Ordnance Office, Tower.
Birkbeck, George, M.D.
Bottman, Edward.
Bostock, John, M.D. On Galvanism, Respiration, etc.
Bramah, Timothy.
BRANDE, Wm. T. Chymist.
Brown, Capt. Samuel. Inventor of Iron Cables.
BRUNEL, Sir M. J.
Children, J. C. British Museum.
―――― do.
―――― do.
Clissold, F. *a*.
Colby, Captain. "Trigonometrical Survey." *a*.
CONGREVE. Sir Willam. *a*.
Cowper, Edward. Inventor of the Steam Printing Machine.
DAVY, Sir Humphry. Portrait. *a*.
FARADAY, Michael.
―――― do.
Farey, John
FRANKLIN, Dr. Benjamin. 2 portraits.
Greenough, G. B. Geologist.
Harrison, Thomas. Royal Institution
Hatchett, Charles. Numerous Treatises on Scientific Subjects. *a*.
Henry, William. Chymist. Elements of Experimental Chymistry.
Horsburgh, James. Several works on Hydrography.
Horspath, Thomas.
Jackson, John.
Kater, Capt. Henry. On Hygrometry, the Pendulum, etc.
Lees, William. Ordnance Office, Tower. *a*.
Leslie, John. Professor at Edinburgh. Numerous Works.
McCullock, John. "System of Geology and Theory of the Earth," etc.
Manly, Geo. Wm. Miscellaneous Writer.

MASKELYNE, Nevil. Astronomer Royal. Numerous works on Astronomy. Portrait.
Millington, John. Lectures on Mechanics.
Moore, Daniel, F.R.S. On British Grasses.
Morrison, James W. Of the Mint. *a*.
Murray, John. Elements of Chymistry and other works.
NEWTON, Sir Isaac. Portrait only.
NICHOLSON, William. Numerous Scientific and other works.
Parker, Samuel. Chymist. Portrait.
Perkins, Jacob. *a*.
Phillips, William. Works on Mineralogy and Geology.
―――― Richard. Chymist.
Pittruci, B. Medalist.
Pond, John. Astronomer.
Prout, William. Animal Chymistry.
RENNIE, John, F.R.S. Portrait.
―――― George.
―――― Sir John.
―――― James.
ROGET, Peter M., F.R.S. On Electricity, Galvanism, etc. *a*.
RUMFORD, Count. Portrait. *a*.
Sadler, John. Lecturer.
Taylor, John. On Mining.
―――― Richard. Printer.
TELFORD, Thomas. Civil Engineer.
Thomson, Thomas. Numerous works on Chemistry, etc.
Walker, William. Lecturer. Port. *a*.
―――― Ralph. Several Treatises on Magnet. Portrait.
WATT, James. Portrait.
―――― James, Jr.
―――― do.
Webster, Thomas. Geologist.
Wallaston, Dr. Frederick William.
Young, Dr. Thos. Lectures on Natural Philosophy and other works.

―――――

V,OLUME XXVIII.

Engravers.

Agar, J. S. *a*.
Armstrong, Cosmo.
Bartolozzi, Jr.

Basire, James.
——— James, Jr.
Blore, Edward. Now an Architect.
Bragg, Thomas.
Branston, Robert.
Bromley, William. *a.*
Byrne, William. *a.*
Cardon, Anthony.
Chamberlaine, W. *a.*
Cook. Tichfield Street. *a.*
Cooke, William B.
——— George.
——— do.
Corner, John.
——— do.
Earlom, Richard.
Engleheart, Francis.
Evans, William.
Finden, William.
Freeman, Samuel.
Fry, William Thomas.
Girten, John.
Gladwin, George.
Golding, Richard.
Greig, John.
Havell, D.
Heath, James. Portrait. *a.*
Holl, William.
Holloway, Thomas.
Landseer, John.
LeKeux, Henry.
——— John.
Lowry, Wilson. Portrait.
Mackenzie, R. *a.*
Medland, Thomas.
Meyer, Henry.
——— do.
Milton, Thomas. *a.*
Moses, Henry. *a.*
Moss, Henry.
Ogborne, John.
Picart, Charles.
——— do. *a.*
Pye, John.
Pye, Charles.
Rawle, S.
——— S.
Schiavonetti, L. *a.*
——— N. *a.*

Reynolds, S. W.
Scott, John.
——— do.
Scriven, Edward.
Sharp, William. Portrait.
Sherlock, W. P.
Skelton, Joseph.
Smith, John Thos. British Museum.
Storer, James.
——— Henry S.
Strange, Lady, wife of Sir. *a.*
Thomson, P.
Thomkins, P. Wm.
Turner, Charles.
Warren, Charles. *a.*
——— do.
Watson, Caroline. *a.*
Worthington. *a.*

VOLUME XXIX.
Merchants.

Anderdon, John L. West India Merchant and Collector of Autog'hs.
Angerstein, John Julius. Portrait. *a.*
Antrobius, Edward. Banker.
Atkins, John. Lord Mayor in 1819. Portrait.
Attwood, J. Banker. *a.*
Barclay, George.
——— David. *a.*
Baring, Sir Thomas. Now Lord Ashburton.
Blades. Sheriff. Ludgate Hill. *a.*
Bonar, Thomson. *a.*
Bosanquet, Henry. Merchant. *a.*
——— William. *a.*
Boydell, Josiah.
Bridges, George. Lord Mayor. Port.
Brown, Anthony.
——— Timothy.
Burchell, William. *a.*
Cohen, Solomon. *l. s.*
Combe, Harvey Christian. *a.*
Cotton, William.
——— William, his son.
Cotton, Joseph. East India Director.
Coutts, Thomas. Banker. Portrait.

Curtis, Sir Wm., M.P. Banker. Port.
——— William, Jr.
Davison, Alexander. Lord Nelson's Agent. *a.*
Denison, P. *a.*
Domville.
Eamer, Sir John. *a.*
Farquhar, Robert. Purchaser Fonthill Abbey.
Favell, Samuel.
Frazen, Sir William. *a.*
Fry, William. Banker. *a.*
Gostling, S. Banker. *a.*
Grant, C. India Director. *a.*
Haldimand, William, M.P. *a.*
Hankey, Thomas. Banker.
——— William A.
Harman, Jeremiah.
Harries. Banker. *a.*
Heygate, William. Lord Mayor. Port.
——— do. *a.*
Hibbert, George. West India Merch.
Hoare, Henry. Banker.
——— do.
Hollingworth, Claudius Stephen. Lord Mayor. Portrait.
Inglis, James.
Innes, John.
Hunter, Claudius Stephen. Lord Mayor. Portrait.
Jackson, Sir John. E. I. Director. *a.*
Mainwaring, William Boulton. *a.*
Maitland, J. *a.*
——— do.
Manning, William. W. I. Merchant.
Pares. Banker. *a.*
Perring. *a.*
Price, Sir Charles. *a.*
——— Lady Price, his wife.
Raikes, Job Matthew. *a.*
Rawlins, Sir William. *a.*
Robarts, William P. Banker.
Rogers, Henry. do.
Samuda, David.
Sandeman, George.
Saunders, James.
Shaw, Sir Jas. Lord Mayor. Port. *a.*
Smith, John. Banker. *a.*

Thornton, Henry.
——— Samuel.
——— Robert.
——— John.
Towgood, John. Banker.
Turner, Charles Hampton. *a.*
——— do.
Vaughan, William. American Merch't.
Vaux, Jasper. *a.*
Waithman, Robert. Lord Mayor.
Watson, Brook. Lord Mayor.
Wigram, Sir Robert. *l. s.*
Wilson, Thomas, M.P., for London.
Wood, Matthew. Lord Mayor. Port. *a.*
——— He destroyed himself on the Beach at Worthing.

VOLUME XXX.
Eminent Women.

Aikin, Lucy. Historian.
Appleton, Elizabeth. Novelist.
Baillie, Anne. *a.*
Barbauld, Anne L. Portrait. *a.*
Barrett, Elizabeth B. (Mrs. Browning.)
Beckedorff, Mrs. Queen Charlotte's Establishment. *a.*
Benger, Elizabeth. Biographer.
——— do. *a.*
Benson, Miss. Novelist. *a.*
Bowdler, Harriet M. Poems, Essays, etc.
Brooke, Frances. Novelist. Portrait.
Bryan, Margaret. "System of Astronomy," and other Scientific Works. Portrait. *a.*
——— do. *a.*
Burney, Sarah H. Novelist. *a.*
B. Miss. Anonymous. *a.*
Carter, Elizabeth. Poems, Translations, etc. Portrait.
Butler, Lady Eleanor.
Dacre, Lady Barbarina Wilmot. Nov't.
Damer, Hon. Anne Seymour. Eminent as a Sculptor, and for her general accomplishments. Portrait.
Edgeworth, Mary. *a.*
Evelyn, Lady M.

FRY, Elizabeth. Portrait. *a*.
Graham, Maria. "Journal of a Residence in India."
Hackett, Maria. Poetess.
HEMANS, Felicia.
Holderness, Mary. "Travels in Tartary," etc.
Holford, Margaret. Poems. *a*.
HOFLAND, Mrs. B. Portrait.
Hunter, Miss. "Miscellanies."
Hutton, Chtherine. Novelist.
LAMB, Lady Carstone. Portrait. *a*.
Leadbeatter, Mary. "Cottage Biography in Ireland."
LINWOOD, Mary. Portrait.
MACAULEY, Elizabeth. Poetess. Port.
MONTAGU, Elizabeth. Portrait.
MORE, Hannah. Two portraits.
MORGAN, Lady Sydney. Two portraits.
OPIE, Amelia. Portrait. *a*.
—— do. *a*.
PARDOE, Julia S. Writer of History, Travels, etc.
Parsons, Jane. Novel Writer.
Pilkington, Mary. Portrait.
PORTER, Jane. Novelist. Portrait. *a*.
Serres, Olivia. Miscellaneous Writer.
SHERIDAN, Mrs. (Ogle). Portrait. *a*.
SMITH, Charlotte. Poetess and Novelist. Portrait.
Spence, Elizabeth Isabella. Novels and Travels. Portrait.
Butler, Lady Caroline. *a*.
Starke, Mary.
Trimmer, Sarah. Portrait.
Wesley, Sarah.
WILLIAMS, Helen Maria. Miscellaneous Writer. Portrait.

VOLUME XXXI.

Foreign.

Alquier, C.
Automarchi, Fr. Napoleon's Surgeon at St. Helena.
Artaud.
Aucher, Dr. Pasquale. *l. s.*

Auger, L. S. "Critique" and Miscellaneous Writer.
Barriere, F. S.
BERRYER, M.
BERTRAND-MOLEVILLE. Louis Sixteenth's Minister, Historian, etc. *a*.
Boettiger, Charles.
BOINVILLIERS. Poet.
Boissonade.
Boissy d'Anglos. Statesman.
BOUILLY. Author.
Buchon, J. A.
Brochart de Villiers.
Brühl, Countess. *a*.
Calbo, A.
Capelle, M.
Rossi, Jos. Chs. Aurele. Italian Poet, Diplomatist, etc., in the French Service for thirty-five years. *a*.
Catellan. Orator.
Caumont, Count of.
Chaintre.
CHARTRES, Duke of.
Chenevix, R.
COMTE, Augustus. Founder of "Positive Theology." *a*.
CONSTANT, Benjamin.
Corray. Hellenhist.
D'ALEMBERT, John Le Rond. Port. *a*.
Debreuil, P. Orator.
De Gerando.
DENON, Dominique Vivant. Portrait.
DIDEROT, Dennis. *a*.
Dugar, Mont-bel.
Duillier, J. C. Fatio De.
Dumouchel.
DUMOURIER, General Charles Francois. Portrait. *a*.
DUPIN, Charles.
Edmont. Poet.
Fauchat. do.
Felitz. Author.
FOSCOLO, Ugo. Italian Poet.
Gail. Translator.
—— Madame. Composer.
GALL, Dr. F. J. Portrait.
Gauthier. Lecturer. *a*.
GAY, Madame. Authoress. *a*.

Haber, E. C. Poet.
Genlis, Madame De. Portrait.
Ghiès, Hussan d'. Tripoline Ambassador. a.
Ginguené.
Gramont, Duke de. a.
Gregoire, Henri, Count. Bishop of Blois. A leading and eccentric character in the French Revolution; better known as "L'Abbe Grégoire."
Harcourt, Duke of. a.
Haüy. Mineralogist.
Humboldt, Frederic Alex'r, Baron Von.
Jacobi, Kloest, Baron. Ambassador. a.
Jordan, Camille. Statesman.
Jerusalem, John Frederick William Commonly "Abbe." A celebrated German Luther'n Divine.
Jouamini, J.
Kerivalant. Poet.
—— do. stanzas.
Laffon-Ladebat, André Daniel. Banker, and distinguished Statesman.
Lafont, Madame. Singer. a.
Lallemand, General. a.
Langlès. Orientalist.
Lasteyrie, Count de. Introduced Lithography into France.
Leibnitz, Gottfried Wilhelm. Port. a.
Mallet du Pan. Political Writer.
Maltzahn, Baron. Prussian Minister. a.
Malte-Brun. Geographer.
Michaud, J. C. Poet, Historian, Miscellaneous Writer.
Michot, A. Inimitable Low Comic.
Millin, A. L. Antiquary.
Mina. Spanish General and Patriot. Portrait.
Mirabeau, Count de.

Mollieu. Statesman.
Montandos, Madame de.
Montolieu, Madame de.
Musset, V. Miscellaneous Writer.
Naldi, Sebastian. A celebrated Italian Singer, killed in Paris. Port.
Ocheda, Tho. de. Bibliographer. a.
Panin, Count de. Minister. a.
Pettier, Political Writer.
Pixedecourt, Réné Charles G. de. Writer of 100 Plays, besides other Works.
Pistrucci, Ferdinando del. Italian Judge, and Political Writer.
Ravizotti. Grammarian. a.
Renouard. Bibliographer.
Rogueford, R.
Richelieu, Marshal Duke of. To Voltaire. a.
Royau, Marquis de. Historian. a.
Sallion de Nantes. Poet.
Santon de Santa Rosa, Count. Statesman.
Sequier, Baron. a.
Sicard, The Abbé. a.
Staël, Madame de. Portrait.
—— Baron de, her husband.
—— Abortine, Duchess de Broglie, her daughter.
Thiebault de Barnard.
Valentinois, Duchess of. Mistress of Louis XVI. a.
Vanderbourg.
Van Swinden, J. H.
Victor, J. B. de St. Poet.
Vincent de Paul, St.
Volney, C. F. C. Portrait.
Voltaire. Portrait.
Zenobio, Count. Ambassador.
Spurzheim, Dr. a.

Unless a satisfactory price is offered for the set as a whole, each volume will be sold separately.

308 Owen (Rev. John). A Divine of the Church of England.
  A L S   3 pp, 8vo   Feb. 9th, 1814

309 Oxberry (W.) A L S Short Letter

ALFREY (John G.)   Secretary of Massachusetts.
   A L S 4to   1846

311 PALMERSTON (Lord). *A N* 3d person   1816

312 PARDOE (Miss M. H.) Authoress   *A N S*

313 PARK (J. A.) Eminent English Lawyer. *A N S* 1824

314 PARKER (Geo.) Fourth Earl of Macclesfield, D.C.L. and F.R.S. *A N* 3d person

315 PARKMAN (Hon. Francis). Historian. *A L S* 12mo
                                                                                1852

316 PARRIS (   ). Receipt Signed for a Prisoner at the prison " la Concergerie."   July 4th, 1792

317 PARRY (Capt. E. W., R. N.) *A N* 3d person. *Portrait*

318 PARSONS (William). Earl of Rosse, Baron Oxmantown.
                                                                                A L S

319 PASCALIS (LE DOCTEUR FELIX). Anecdote Historique relative au Tassemblement du *Trou-Coffi*, dans le district de la Paroisse de Léogane, Decembre, 1791. Isle St. Dominique. Autograph, 32 pp, with certificates from the French Consul, D'Espinville, at New York, that it is correct, etc.

320 PEARSON (Dr. George, M.D. and F.R.S.)   *A N S*

321 PEPOLI (Count). Italian Patriot. *A L S* 1 p, French

322 PEPOLI (Countess). Wife of the Italian Patriot Count Pepoli. *A N* 3d person

323 PERCEVAL (Chas. George). Baron Ardin. *A N* 3d person

324 PHILLIP (Thomas, R. A.)   *A L S*

325 PICKERING (J.)   *A L S*

326 PICKERING (TIMOTHY). U. S. Secretary of State
   A L S 4to   1813

327 PIKE (Albert). Poet. *A L S* 4to

328 PINCKNEY (Charles Colesworth). *A L S* 3 pp, 4to.

329 PINDER (Miss Susan). Authoress. *A N S*

330 PITT (WILLIAM, Right Hon.) Treasury Warrant. *S* Portrait.

331 POINSETT (J. R.) *A L S* 4 pp, 4to.   1835

332 PORTEUS (Rev. Beilby). Bishop of London. *A N* 3d person. *Portrait.*

333 PRANDI (V.) Translator of Andryane, etc. *A N S* 1839

334 PRESTON (Hon. Wm.) U. S. Senator from South Carolina. *A L S* 12mo.

335 PRINCESSE DE CHIMAY (Mm. Tallien). *A N S* 8vo.

336 PROCTOR (B. W.), alias Barry Cornwall. *A L S.*

337 PROVISIONAL RETURNS. 1788. 2.

338 PUTNAM (Gen. Rufus). Member U. S. Assembly, 1787. Bill signed.

339 PYE (C.) Engraver.   *A L S*

340 PYE (John).   *A L S*

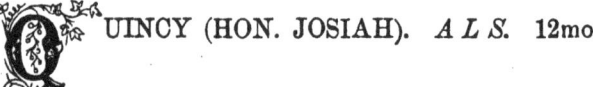
UINCY (HON. JOSIAH). *A L S.* 12mo.

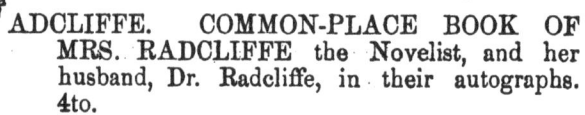
ADCLIFFE. COMMON-PLACE BOOK OF MRS. RADCLIFFE the Novelist, and her husband, Dr. Radcliffe, in their autographs. 4to.

343 RAMSAY (Allan). JOURNAL OF THE EASY CLUB. Containing the History and Proceedings of that Modern Society, for their first three years. With several Poems. 1715 –'26, quarto, *half calf.*

Except a few printed poems, the whole volume is autographic. Allan Ramsay was born in 1686; died 1757. He is a remarkable instance of uncultivated genius rising from the humblest station in life to high eminence as a poet. He was known to fame, and his company courted by the best society in Edinburgh, long before he gave up his trade of wig-maker. His earliest poem published was an Address, in 1712, to his fellow-members of the "Easy Club," of which he was one of the founders. "It was composed of young men of ability, who assembled together to spend the evening in hilarity. Each member was known by the name of some man of distinction, which he chose from a supposed resemblance to himself in talents or pursuits." The number was limited to twelve. The "Journal" contains poems by several of its members: the best by Ramsay.

344 RAMSAY (David). Physician and Historian. *A L S.* 2pp, 4to, *Portrait.* 1787

Letter to Rev. W. Morse offering to answer his queries, and wishing his settlement as co-partner with Mr. Hollingshead.

345 RAMSAY (David). *A N S.* 1785

346 RENNIE (George). Son of Sir John Rennie. *A L S.* In relation to the Motto of a Medal to his father. Royal Mint. 1821

347 RENNIE (James). Lecturer and Author. *A L S.*

348 RICHARDSON (G. F.) Author, Geology. *A L S.* 2 pp, 12mo.

349 RICHELIEU (ARMAND I. DU PLESSIS). Cardinal and Minister of State. *D S on vellum, old portrait, very rare.*

350 ROBESPIERRE, brother of Maximilian, Guillotined with him, 1794. *D S. Very rare.*

351 ROBY (J. S.) *A L S.* 12mo.

352 RODNEY (Cæsar). Signer of Declaration. *A L S.* 1 p, 4to. 1782

353 RODNEY (George). Third Baron. *A N* 3d person. *Mounted.*

354 ROLAND LA PLATIERE (Jean Marie). Minister of the Interior, 1792. Proscribed 1793. On hearing of the Condemnation of his Wife he deliberately stabbed himself, Nov. 15th, 1793. *A L S*

355 ROSE (Right Hon. Geo.) Statesman and Political Writer. *A N*

356 ROSE (William Stewart). *A N* 3d person.

357 ROSS (Capt. John). *A L S*

358 ROUSSEAU (J. J.) Poet. *A L S* 1 page, 4to. *With rare old portrait, good specimen.*
Montmorenci, Feb. 10th, 1762

Interesting Letter to his Printer respecting his Works.

359 ROYT (P. M.) *A N S*

ABINE (Joseph, F.R.S.) *A N S*

361 SAMUEL (E.) Bishop of Norwich. *A L S* 3 pp, 12mo 1816

362 SCOMBERG (Henry de). Marshal of France. *D S Vellum* 1619

363 SCORESBY (Wm., Jr.) Arctic Voyager. *A N S*

364 SCOTT (SIR WALTER). THE HISTORY OF SCOTLAND. Vol. one, Original Manuscript, entirely in the author's Autograph. Vols. two and three, Original Manuscript dictated by the author to his friend, Laidlaw, and in his Autograph, with many additions in the Autograph of the author. Vol. four, The History of Scotland—proofs corrected by the author—in all 4 vols. Vol. 1, 4to, *half calf*, the balance folio, *half calf.*
None of the volumes are complete.

365 SCOTT (SIR WALTER). Fac-Simile. *A L S.* 1½ p, 4to. April 23d, 1813

366 SCOTT (W.) Lord Stowell. *A N S*

367 SEDGWICK (Catherine M.) Authoress. *A L S.* 3 pp, 4to. *Portrait.*

368 SERRURIER (Jeaume-Mathieu Philberti). Senateur et Governeur des Invalides. Born 1742, died 1819. *A L S.* 1 p, folio. 1808

369 SEVIGNÉ. *A L S.* 2 pp.

370 SERVAN (Le Chr. de). *A L S.* Small 4to, 1 p. 1788

371 SEWARD (William, F.R.S. and A.S.S.) A Biographical Writer. *A N S*

372 SHERIDAN (R. B.) Distinguished as a Statesman, Wit, and Dramatist. *A N S.* Slightly stained.

373 SIGNATURES OF STATESMEN.—Viz : George Ashmun, William Appleton, David Crocket, S. A. Douglass, etc., etc., Fastened on 4to sheet. 16.

375 SINCLAIR (Sir John), of Ulster. Philanthropist. *A O N* 3d person

376 SMIRKE (Robert), R. A. *A L S.* April 3d 1812

377 SMITH (James). Poet. *A L S.*

378 SMITH (Dr. J. Pye). *A L S.* 3 pp, 8vo April 2d, 1820

379 SOANE (John). Artist. *A L S.*

380 SOUTHEY, Wordsworth, Rogers, etc. *A E.* 14

381 SOUTHEY (Robert). MEMOIRES DE LA CAMPAGNE EN PORTUGAL. L'an 1762. Entirely in his autograph. Written in French. 12mo, *calf*

    A very neat transcript.

382 SOUTHWELL (Edward). COLLECTIONS E TERENTIO. With his own Translation of the Extracts, in manuscript. 1717. Small, 4to, *parchment.* 92 pp

383 SPARKS (Jared). Biographer. *A L S.* 3 pp, 4to 1844

384 SPARKS (Jared). Author. *A L S. Half*, 4to

385 STANHOPE (Philip Henry). Fourth Earl of Stanhope.
A L S. Aug. 13th, 1824

386 STAUNTON (Sir George Leonard). Secretary to Macartney, Embassador to China, 1791. Born, 1737. Died, 1810.

387 STEEL (Sir Richard). Celebrated Essayist and Dramatic Writer. Very rare. *A L S.* 4to 1712

388 STEPHENSON (Hon. A.) *A L S.* 1 p, 4to 1860

389 STERNE (Laurence). ORIGINAL MS. of "THE FRAGMENT." 8vo

Entirely autograph, and quite perfect. It differs from the printed copies, especially in the coarser passages. Written in a remarkably clear hand.

390 STEUBEN (Major Gen. : Baron). *A O S.* For Sixty Dollars. Old Portrait.

391 STODDARD (Thomas). An Eminent English Artist. *A L S.*

392 STRONG (Caleb). Governor of Massachusetts. 4to, 1802

393 SULLY (Maximilian de Bethune, Duc de). Ministre de Henri IV. One of the greatest Ministers of France, of the Reformed Religion. Very fine specimen.

394 TALFOURD (T. N.) *A L S.* 2pp, 4to. Portrait.

395 TALFOURD (T. N.) Author. *A N S.*

396 TALLEYRAND (C. M. De). Celebrated Diplomatist. Very good and rare specimen.

397 THANE'S BRITISH AUTOGRAPHY. A Collection of Authentic Portraits and fac-similes of the hand-writing of

Royal and Illustrious Personages. Containing upwards of 250 fine Portraits, and as many Autographs and Seals, with Bibliographical Memoirs. 3 vols. 4to, *half morocco* 1819

<small>One of the most valuable and interesting collections of Autographs and Portraits ever published—the portraits on tinted paper—many from originals never before engraved, and not to be found in any other publication.</small>

398 THOMAS (Seth). One of the Earliest Printers in the United States. Bill S. Very rare.

399 THOMPSON (John R.) Verses on Crawford's Equestrian Statue of Washington, in his own hand, with signature. 3 pp

400 THOMSON (Mrs.) Authoress. *A S.* 3d person.

401 TOMLINE (Geo. Prettyman). Bishop of Lincoln and Winchester. *A N S.*

402 TOMPKINS (D. D.) Vice President of the United States. *L S.* 1 p, 4to. Portrait. *Mounted.*

403 TUPPER (Martin F.) Poet. *A L S.* 3 pp, 12mo. Portrait.

404 TURENNE (Henry de la D'Auvergne : Viscount). The Illustrious French Marshal, Killed by a Cannon Ball, July 27th, 1675. *A L S.* 1 p. Small 4to

405 TURNER (The.) *A L S.*

406 TYLER (JOHN). Ex-President U. S. *A L S.* 2 pp. 4to. 1853

407 VAN MILDAT (RT. REV. WILLIAM). Bishop of Llandaff. *A L S.* Signed W. Llandaff. 1824

408 VILLIERS (Sarah Sophia; Lady Jersey.) *A N.* 3d person.

WADSWORTH (COM. ALEX. S.) *A L S.* 1 p. 4to. 1840

410 WARE (Henry, Jr.) Author. *A L S.* 3 pp. 12mo.

411 WARRINGTON (Commodore L., U. S. N.) *L S.* 1 p. 4to.

412 WASHINGTON (GEO.) *L S.* To his nephew, Bushrod Washington. 4to. Neatly repaired. 1796

413 WASHINGTON (Geo. V.) Nephew to Gen. Washington. *A L S.* 1 p. folio. 1827

414 WAUGH (Rev. Alex., D.D.), of the Church of Scotland. *A L S.* 1822

415 WAY (John Allan). Wrote a work concerning the Life of Sir William Wallace, to which this letter refers. *A L S.*

416 WEBSTER (Daniel). *A N S* and franked. *Portrait.*

417 WEBSTER (Daniel). *A N.*, 3d person. *Portrait.*

418 WEED (Thurlow). Editor. *A L S.* 1 p. 12mo. 1847

— 419 WHITE (J. Blanco). *A L S.* 1824

420 WHIFFEN (J. H.) Celebrated Quaker Poet. *A N S.*

— 421 WILBERFORCE (W.) Philanthropist. *A L S.* 3 pp. 12mo.

422 WILCOX (Rev. J.) Episcopal Clergyman. *A L S.* 3 pp. 8vo. 1824

423 WILKIE (SIR DAVID). Celebrated Painter. *A L S.* 1823

424 WILKS (Rev. Mark), and eight others. 9

425 WINTER (Rev. Robt., D.D.) Dissenting Minister. Writer of several works on Religious Subjects. *A L S.* Dec. 12th, 1817

426 WINTHROP (Robert C.) U. S. Senator from Massachusetts.
A L S. 3 pp. 4to.

427 WOODBURY (Hon. Levi). Judge Supreme Court U. S.
A L S. 1 p. 4to. *Portrait.* 1838

428 WRIGHT (George). A L S. 3 pp., torn. 1759

429 WRIGHT (J. C.) Translator of Dante. A L S. 6 pp.
Small 4to.

YORKE (CHARLES PHILIP). Earl of Hardwicke.
A N., 3d person.

SCHOKKE (HENRY). Author. A L S. with translation to letter.

432 CONTINENTAL Money. Bill of Thirty Dollars. State of
Georgia. 1778

433 CONTINENTAL Money. Package, with which are Two Bills Mass. State Lottery. Assignat (10 sous), Napoleon's time. Signed by Guyon.

434 WARRANT, Treasury. State of Massachusetts. With various Autograph Signatures. April 2d, 1777

435 WARRANT, Treasury. State of Massachusetts. With various Autograph Signatures. April 10th, 1777

Lightning Source UK Ltd.
Milton Keynes UK
UKHW011051190522
403228UK00003B/311